# NIGHT SHOW

She blinked her eyes open and saw her hands on her lap. They were bound together. The pale rope angled upward to the banister. She was seated on the third stair, her feet resting on the floor. Her ankles were tied together.

So, they'd done it. They'd tied her up, and left her here all alone.

'Guys? Hey, look, I know you're here.'

She waited. The house was silent. Somewhere above Linda, a board creaked.

She flung herself away from the railing. Ignoring the pain in her wrists, she tugged furiously. The rope snapped. She dropped. Her back and head pounded on the floor. A movement drew her eyes to the top of the stairs. A dim figure stood in the darkness.

Linda's breath burst out as if she'd been punched in the stomach.

An arm of the figure swung forward. A pale object seemed to break off. It hung in the air, fell, and hit the stairs midway down with a harsh thud. She ached to throw herself out of its path. She tore at the rope round her ankles. The knot opened as the thing thumped off the final stair and rolled against her rump. A single, wide eye peered through the crevice between her legs . . .

**By Richard Laymon published
by New English Library:**

**BEWARE
ALLHALLOWS EVE
BEASTHOUSE**

# Night Show

---

# Richard Laymon

**NEW ENGLISH LIBRARY**
Hodder and Stoughton

A New English Library
Original Publication, 1984

Copyright © 1984 by Richard
Laymon

First NEL Paperback Edition
December 1984

Reissued 1992
*Fourth impression 1993*

British Library CIP Data

Laymon, Richard
  Night show.
  I. Title
813'54[F]      PS3562.A95/

ISBN 0 450 05706 2

Printed and bound in Great Britain
for Hodder and Stoughton Paper-
backs, a division of Hodder and
Stoughton Ltd., Mill Road, Dunton
Green, Sevenoaks, Kent TN13 2YA
(Editorial Office: 47 Bedford
Square, London WC1B 3DP) by
Clays Ltd., St Ives plc.

# ONE

A CAR slowed down, keeping pace with Linda. She didn't look. She walked faster, hugging the books more tightly against her chest.

She wished, now, that she had accepted her father's offer to pick her up. But she'd hoped to run into Hal Walker at the library. She had waited at a table near the entrance, trying to study, her heart racing each time the door opened. Betty came in. Janice and Bill came in. The nurd, Tony, came in and made a pest out of himself until she told him to get lost. But Hal never showed up.

'Hey Linda, want a ride?'

Her head snapped toward the car. A dumpy old station wagon. Tony's car. She might've known. She counted three vague figures in the front seat.

'How about it?' a boy called through the open window.

'Bug off.'

'Aw, come on.'

She picked up her pace, but the car stayed beside her.

'Think you're hot shit.'

She ignored the remark, and tried to place the voice. Not Tony. This had to be one of his jerk-off friends. Maybe Joel Howard, or Duncan Brady, or Arnold Watson. A bunch of scuzzy misfits.

'Get out of here!' she yelled.

'Don't think so,' said the boy at the window.

'Look guys, you're gonna be in big trouble if you don't cut it out.'

'Cut what out?'

'Her tongue?' asked a different voice.

She reached the corner and stepped off the curb. The station wagon swung in front of her.

'I'm warning you . . .'

Her voice stopped as the door flew open.

Two boys leaped out. In the streetlight, she glimpsed their twisted, flattened faces. She whirled around to run, but even as she sprang for the curb an arm hooked her waist. Her books tumbled. She was yanked backwards. She tried to yell. A hand clutched her mouth, mashing her lips into her teeth. She squirmed and kicked. A boy lunged against her legs, grabbed them and lifted.

She was carried to the car. The third boy swung open the tail door. The other two wrestled her inside, and the door thunked shut.

She was in darkness, one boy under her back, one on top of her legs. She tried to pry the arm loose from her belly. The hand on her mouth pinched her nostrils shut. She couldn't breathe. The car lurched forward. She tugged at the smothering hand. The other arm eased its clench, and a fist hammered her belly. She felt as if a bomb had exploded, bursting her lungs and heart.

'Lay still.'

She grabbed her chest, struggling to breathe. The boy's hands, she realised, had moved down to her hips. He was holding her firmly, but no longer crushing her.

'You okay?' asked the boy on her legs.

She couldn't answer.

'You weren't supposed to hurt her, asshole.'

'She was fighting me,' said the one beneath her. She recognized his whiny voice – Arnold Watson – and decided she might be better off keeping the knowledge to herself. At least until she got away.

Arnold held her steady as the car took a corner fast.

She found that she could breathe again, though her lungs still ached. 'Let me go,' she said. 'Please.'

Arnold laughed, his belly shaking under her back.

'What do you *want*?'

'You,' he said. 'And we've got you, haven't we? The one and only Linda Allison.'

'Please, just let me go. I promise I'll never speak a word. Honest.'

'You had your chance.'

'Huh?'

'Should've been nice when you had the chance. Think you're hot shit, always dumping on us.'

'I don't either. I never . . .'

'We've got feelings, you know. The question is, do *you*?'

'Of course I do. For godsake . . . !'

'You're gonna get it, now.'

'What are you . . . ?' She couldn't bring herself to finish, this time; she didn't want to hear the answer.

'We've got plans for you.'

'No. Please. Just let me go. Please!'

'Real interesting plans.'

'Tell her,' said the boy on her legs.

'Hell no. Let her worry about it. Right?'

'Right,' said the driver. 'She'll think of all kinds of neat stuff.' Though the voice was low and husky, apparently to disguise it, she knew it came from Tony. 'What do you think we'll do to you, huh, bitch?'

'Please. Just let me go. I'm sorry if I hurt your feelings.'

'Too late for sorry.'

'Please.'

'Who knows?' Tony said. 'Maybe you'll get yourself raped, or tortured. Maybe your pretty face is gonna get all fucked up with battery acid or a knife. How would you like that?'

Linda started to cry.

'Maybe you'll get cut up into little tiny pieces: first your toes and fingers, then maybe those nice big tits . . .'

'Come on, stop it,' said the boy on her legs.

Tony laughed. 'Bet you can feel that knife, right now, slicing into your . . .'

'Don't listen to him. We're not going to hurt you.'

'Don't count on it.'

'Hey, you said we'd just . . .'

'I know, I know.'

7

'Go ahead and tell her,' Arnold said.

'Okay okay. Here's what's really gonna happen. You know the old Freeman house?'

'Yes,' she sobbed, and wiped the tears from her face.

'It's still deserted. Nobody'll touch the place. It's supposed to be haunted. They say the ghosts of all those bodies moan inside the walls where crazy Jasper plastered them up, and that Jasper himself walks the house at night looking for fresh young girls to chop. Girls just like you.'

'He's dead,' Linda muttered.

'It's his ghost,' Arnold whispered. 'And he wants *you*.'

'Fun, huh?' asked Tony. 'Nice place to spend the night.'

'You're not . . . !'

'Oh yes we are.'

Her dread was mixed with relief. Tony had talked of rape and torture just to scare her. All they really intended was to leave her alone in the Freeman house.

All.

Oh God!

But Jasper'd hanged himself in jail. No reason to fear him.

No such thing as ghosts.

But to be alone in the very house . . .

'You're crazy,' Linda muttered.

'Yeah,' Tony said. 'Real crazy. But not half as crazy as old Jasper.' She felt the car slow down and turned. 'Here we are. Your home away from home.'

It stopped. Tony climbed out. He opened the tailgate, and Linda was dragged feet first from the car. The boys stood her up and held her steady. Their faces, in the darkness, were weirdly stretched and distorted, their hair flat as if painted on. She realised, now, that the effect was caused by nylon stocking masks. Knowing the cause, however, didn't help. She felt as if the boys were grotesque strangers only pretending to be Tony and Arnold and – who was the other, Joel?

'Let's go,' said the one with Tony's voice. He started toward the gate of the low, picket fence. The other boys, one on each arm, forced Linda ahead.

8

The Freeman house looked similar to many of the older homes in Claymore, a two-story frame structure with a front porch, and a picture window looking out from the living room. Someone had kept it up. The lawn was trim. Only the shuttered upstairs windows and the FOR SALE, LELAND REALTORS sign hinted that it stood vacant.

The hinges groaned as Tony pushed open the gate. 'Wonder if Jasper heard that,' he whispered.

Arnold laughed softly, but his fingers dug into Linda's upper arm. He's frightened, she thought. He doesn't want to go in there any more than I do.

She looked to the right. In that direction was only the golf course, deserted now, a sprinkler hissing on the nearest green. To the left was the abandoned Benson house.

No help from the rear, either. Across the street, she knew, was only the bait and tackle shop – closed for the night.

The boys forced her along the walkway, up the wooden stairs, onto the porch. She expected the front door to be locked, but Tony turned the knob and pushed it wide open.

They must've been here before, forced their way. . . . They'd planned all this. No spur of the moment decision. They'd plotted, made preparations.

'Anybody home?' Tony called, leaning into the darkness.

'Just us ghosts,' Arnold said, and gave a nervous laugh.

Tony entered. He waved the boys forward, and they guided Linda into the house. The air was cold, as if some of the winter's frost had been trapped inside, the heat of the warm June days kept out. The cold moved up Linda's bare legs, seeped through her thin blouse, brought goosebumps.

Arnold nudged the door. It banged shut, its crash resounding through the house.

'Loud enough to wake the dead,' Tony whispered.

Arnold laughed again.

'Let's hurry up,' said the other boy.

'Nervous?' Tony asked.

'Damn right.'

They walked Linda through the dark foyer. She let each foot down softly, heel first, rolling toward the toe, straining for silence.

All three boys, she realised, were also treading softly. Arnold, holding her right arm, cringed when a floorboard queaked under his weight.

At the foot of the stairway, Tony stoped. His head tilted back as if he were studying the darkness at the top of the stairs. 'Jasper's bedroom was up there,' he whispered. 'They found one of the bodies on his bed. He'd been . . . snacking on it. They say the head was never found.'

'Come on ,' said the boy on Linda's left. Joel. She was sure of that, now. 'Let's get out of here.'

''Fore we freeze our nuts off,' Arnold said.

Tony turned around. He slung the coil of rope off his shoulder. 'Bring her here.'

They tugged Linda's arms. She stamped on Arnold's foot. He grunted and his grip loosened. She jerked her arm free, spinning toward Joel, and drove her elbow into his face. He staggered backwards, letting go. She lunged through the darkness. Her hands clawed the door as footfalls raced toward her. She found the knob. Turned it. Then her back was hit. She slammed forward, her head exploding with pain as it crashed against the door.

A dull ache pulsed behind her eyes. She grimaced, her forehead burning as its skin pulled taut.

She blinked her eyes open, and saw her hands on her lap. They were bound together. The pale rope angled upward to the banister.

She was seated on the third stair, leaning awkwardly against the bars of the railing, her legs sloping down, her feet resting on the floor. Her ankles were tied together.

So, they'd done it. They'd tied her up, and left her here all alone.

Or had they left?

From her position on the stairs, she could see little of the house: the front door, a set of closed doors to the left of the foyer, a corner of the living room and some of its picture window through the entry on the right, and a narrow hallway that ran alongside the staircase. The only light was a pale spill across the living room floor: moonlight slanting in through the window.

No sign of the boys. They'd either left the house or hidden themselves.

'Guys?' she asked, her voice no more than a whisper. 'Hey, look, I know you're here. You're just hiding on me.'

She waited. The house was silent.

She started to shiver. She raised her arms and pressed them tightly against herself for warmth.

'Guys?'

They're probably just out of sight, she thought, huddled together in the living room, nudging each other, trying not to giggle. Sooner or later, they would jump out at her.

'Okay,' she muttered. 'Have it your way.'

The rope, she saw, was looped around the banister and knotted at her wrists. She twisted her arms. Straining her head forward, she found that her teeth could just barely reach the bundle of knots. She bit into it, and tugged. The rope didn't give. Her tongue explored the mass of swirls, felt knot piled upon knot.

Her throat tightened. Her chin started to tremble and she blinked tears from her eyes. She lowered her arms in frustration.

'Come on, guys,' she pleaded. 'You've had your fun. You've taught me my lesson. Now let me go, please.'

Somewhere above Linda, a board creaked. With a gasp, she snapped her head around and looked up the stairway. She stared for a long time, afraid to move.

There was only darkness.

It's just them, she told herself. They didn't hide in the living room, they hid upstairs.

*Fuck off!* she wanted to yell.

But she kept her mouth clamped shut so hard her teeth ached.

She heard another quiet moan of wood. Above, but off to the left. As if someone were sneaking very slowly through the upstairs hallway.

The thought of it raised a whimper in her throat.

She flung herself away from the railing. The tether pulled taut. Ignoring the pain in her wrists, she tugged furiously. The banister squeaked and wobbled a bit. But it held. The rope held.

She drew her legs up, planted her tied feet on the next stair down, dropped to a crouch and sprang at the railing. Her shoulder smashed against the banister. Pain blasted through her body. She recoiled, and fell until the rope yanked at her wrists. It swung her sideways. Her other shoulder slammed into the newel post.

She hung there, numb with pain, her feet still on the second stair, her side against the post, all her weight tugging at her wrists. As she tried to pull herself up, the rope snapped. She dropped. Her back and head pounded the floor.

She lay there, stunned at first. As the pain started to fade, she realised she was free.

Free of the banister!

If she could just untie her feet . . .

Opening her eyes, she raised her head. Her skirt was rumpled around her waist, her panties pale in the darkness, her bare legs angling up to the second stair.

She drew her knees forward. She spread them, reached between them with her tied hands, and felt the knotted rope. As her fingers picked at the coils, a movement drew her eyes to the top of the stairs.

A dim figure stood in the darkness.

Linda's breath burst out as if she'd been punched in the stomach. Her bladder released. She clawed at the knots as the warm fluid spread down her buttocks.

Her eyes stayed on the motionless form. It just stood there.

She jerked a knot loose and kicked her feet. The bonds held. Another knot! She grabbed it, picked it, winced as a fingernail tore off.

An arm of the figure swung forward. A pale object seemed to break off. It hung in the air, fell, and hit the stairs midway down with a harsh thud. Gazing through the gap in her upraised legs, Linda watched it tumble down the remaining stairs. She saw trailing hair, a blur of face. She heard herself whimper again. She ached to throw herself out of its path, but the knot was pulling loose. She tore at the rope. The knot opened as the thing thumped off the final stair and rolled against her rump. A single, wide eye peered through the crevice between her legs. With a shattering scream, Linda kicked her legs free and rolled aside.

She flipped over. On her belly, she glanced from the severed head to the stairway.

The figure was halfway down, walking slowly as if he had all the time in the world. He was naked, boney, and dead pale. A dark beard hung to his chest. He held a long object in his hands – an ax!

Linda shoved herself to her feet. She staggered back, whirled around, and raced for the door. She hit it with her shoulder. She swept down her tied hands, seeking the knob.

Found it!

Her sweaty hands twisted the knob. She dropped back, jerking the door open, crying out as it hammered her knee. Her leg buckled. She dropped hard to her rump, losing her grip on the knob.

The door swung open wide. In the dim light from the porch, she saw the man striding slowly forward. His head was tilted to one side, his face ragged with open sores, his tongue drooping out.

'No!' she shrieked.

He raised the ax high.

With her good leg, Linda thrust herself backward. She slid over the doorsill, and tumbled onto the porch. She rolled, forced herself to her knees, and scrambled for the porch stairs. She hurled herself off them. Clearing the three steps, she caught the walkway with her knuckles and landed flat with an impact that slapped her breasts and thighs and slammed the breath from her lungs. Dazed, she flopped onto her back.

She sat up, and peered into the porch.

The front door of the Freeman house swung shut.


Inside the house, Tony lowered his ax and leaned back against the door. He started to peel the makeup and false beard from his face.

In spite of the chilly air, he wasn't cold.

The tremors that shook his naked body had nothing to do with cold.

They had to do with excitement.

He'd scared himself silly. His heart was thundering, his guts knotted. Touching himself, he felt his gooseflesh, his stiff nipples. His penis was shrunken as if to hide. His scrotum was shriveled the size of a walnut.

My God, what a charge!

Hefting his ax, he made his way across the dark foyer. He stooped, picked up the mannequin head by its hair, and eagerly started up the stairs toward the black upper storey of the house.

# TWO

DANI LARSON leaned forward, bracing her hands on the sill, resting her forehead against the window pane. 'I'm so afraid,' she said. 'Margot, Julie, Alice – all dead.'

She flinched as Michael touched her bare shoulders. 'It's all right, honey,' he whispered. 'You're safe here.' His lips brushed her shoulders.

'Michael, no.'

'I'll help you forget.'

'I don't want to forget. He's out there somewhere, looking for me.'

'Worrying about it won't help.' His hands slipped around to the front of Dani, held her breasts gently through the thin fabric of her nightgown while he nibbled her ear.

She arched her back, moaning as if with pleasure. Suddenly, she gasped. Her eyes bulged. Her mouth jerked open, ready to scream.

'Cut, cut! Beautiful! That's a print!'

'Aw shit,' Michael said. 'Just when I was starting to enjoy it.'

'Should've blown your lines,' Dani said, peeling his fingers off her breasts.

The window flew up, and Roger Weston poked his head inside. 'Beautiful, gang. Lovely. Ready for the splash scene, Dani?'

'We'll set it up.'

'Good kid.'

She turned away, caught Jack's amused look, and shrugged.

'Let's go to it, kid,' Jack told her.

Dani bared her teeth.

'Should've done that to Rog,' he said.

'I don't like to abuse short people. They've got enough

15

troubles.' She picked up her blue windbreaker with MIDNIGHT SCREAMS printed across the back, slipped it on to cover the top, at least, of her sheer nightgown, and snapped it shut.

Then she followed Jack to a corner of the set, where Ingrid stood with her mouth agape and terror in her eyes. The mannequin was a duplicate of Dani: five foot six and slim, with shoulder-length auburn hair, gelatin eyes the same emerald color as her own, and lightly tanned latex skin. It was exact to the tiny scar on its chin, the slightly crooked upper front tooth.

Dani noticed, as she approached, the blatant dark thrust of its nipples through the gown.

She hoped that her own hadn't been so apparent.

They must've been, though. Identical nightgowns, identical breasts. She'd cast them, like the rest of Ingrid, from molds of herself. She'd taken great care, sitting half-naked in her work shop, comparing, trying to find a perfect match of the flesh tone, even though she hadn't known the nightgown would be quite so revealing.

If she hadn't made them so well, maybe she and Ingrid might have both been spared the embarrassment . . .

'Problem?' Jack asked.

'Huh?'

'You look upset.'

'No, it's all right. Just wishing the negligees weren't so transparent.'

'She looks great. You did, too.'

'You're not supposed to notice those things.'

'I'm a man.'

'I'm your boss.'

Jack laughed, and clawed fingers through the side of his dark beard. 'Gonna be the pits, blowing her away.'

'I don't need the competition.'

He wrapped an arm around Ingrid's waist. With a hand bracing her head, he tipped her sideways. Dani grabbed the legs, and lifted.

They carried Ingrid to the window. Dani lowered her feet to the chalk marks, and they set her upright. As Jack left to fetch the other mannequin, the continuity girl held a Polaroid snapshot

rough the window: Dani's final moment with Michael. Using
ie photo as a guide, she arched Ingrid's articulated back and
aced her fingertips on the sill.

Jack set down the Michael mannequin behind Ingrid.

Dani hadn't bothered to rename it, hadn't needed to. Con-
ructing Michael's duplicate, she'd felt none of the eerie dis-
omfort she'd experienced in making her own. Even giving her
odel a rather silly name like Ingrid hadn't been enough to dispel
er uneasiness. At one point, she'd gone so far as to cover
igrid's terrified face with a paper bag.

This morning, she'd let Jack do the dirty work on Ingrid while
ie worked on Michael: stuffing the hollow skulls with blood
icks and calf brains fresh from the butcher. Jack had seemed
luctant, too. But he was a good fellow, always followed instruc-
ons.

Now, they adjusted Michael so he pressed against Ingrid's
ick, his lips against her neck. They raised his arms, placed his
inds over her breasts.

Ingrid, at least, would have no cause for modesty.

Dani checked the final positions against the Polaroid   'All
t,' she called through the window.

Roger strode forward. Dani handed the snapshot out to him.
ie stared at it through his oversized glasses, then studied the
t-up. 'Beautiful, beautiful. Okay, shut the goddamn window.'

Jack lowered the window. He stepped back. He looked at
grid. For an instant, Dani saw a hint of sorrow in his eyes. It
inished, and he winked at Dani. 'This is gonna be good,' he
id.

'Hope so.'

They walked around the wall. From the front, the facade
ipeared to be side of a small, woodframe house. The young
iuple looked frozen behind its window.

The set was crowded, people standing around with coffee
ips, others busy adjusting lights, the sound man in headphones
idling with dials like a HAM operator tuning in to exotic bands,
oger peering through the Paniflex and turning away to instruct
ie weary-looking cameraman.

'I'm off,' Jack said.

17

'Give it your best shot.'

He laughed, and headed away.

While she waited, Dani made her way to the coffee machine. The aluminum container was nearly empty, the fluid black and grainy as it trickled from the spout. In her styrofoam cup, it looked like watery mud. She took a sip and winced at the bitter taste. As she set the cup down, someone reached from behind and squeezed her breasts.

'Hey!' She flung up her arms, forcing the hands off, and whirled.

Michael grinned.

'Don't you *ever* do that again,' she said, barely able to control her rage.

'Whoa!' He raised his open hands as if to ward off an attack. 'So sorry. I just couldn't help myself. My hands have been burning ever since . . .'

'Don't be a jerk.'

'Come on. You enjoyed it.'

'See how you enjoy a punch in the face if you ever try that again.'

'The lady doth protest too much, methinks.'

'Think again.'

'Quiet on the set,' announced a nearby voice. 'Scene forty-four, take one.'

The studio went silent, and a red dome light began to spin. Dani stepped silently away for a better view. Michael stayed at her side.

She spotted Jack near one of the cameras, dressed now in jeans and a parka, a blue ski mask over his head, a shotgun in his hands.

'Action,' Roger said.

Jack ran forward, hunched low in front of the window, brought up the shotgun. But he didn't fire. Instead, he looked over his shoulder. He stood upright and turned around, lowering the weapon.

'Cut, cut, cut!' Roger snapped. 'What the fuck's going on!'

Jack shook his head.

'*Jee*zus! Dani?' Roger twisted to face her. 'Dani, did you tell

18

your boy what's going on? We're making a goddamn movie here. This ain't fun and games, it's the real thing. If he can't pull it off . . .'

'He's fine,' Dani said.

'Bull-fuckin'-shit! You said he could handle it. Nobody touches the goddamn trigger but your boy here. Requires precision, all that bullshit. All right. Okay. Christ! Now let's get it together, huh? That too much to ask?'

'You okay, Jack?' Dani asked, burning from the tirade, embarrassed for herself and Jack, furious with Roger.

Jack nodded.

'Okay,' Roger said in a calm, almost cheerful voice. 'Let's try it again.'

Dani blew out a long breath. She felt drained, as if Roger's tantrum had shaken out all her energy.

'Feathers a bit singed?' Michael whispered.

She glared at him, then turned her attention to Jack.

'The gun loaded?' Michael asked her.

She ignored him.

'Quiet on the set. Scene forty-four, take two.'

Jack was crouched off-camera, waiting.

'Action.'

He ran forward, crouched in front of the window, shouldered the shotgun and fired. The blast stunned Dani's ears. She saw the window blow in. Buckshot slammed into the right side of Ingrid's face, into Michael's forehead as he kissed her neck. Their latex skin disintegrated into pulp. Ingrid's eye vanished. Red, clotted gore exploded from both heads as the two figures flew backwards and vanished from the window.

'Cut, cut! Beautiful!'

'Not bad,' Michael said.

Dani realized she was holding the side of her face, covering her eye. She quickly lowered her hand. It was trembling.

She hurried toward Jack. He was bending down to pick up the spent, red cartridge.

'Great shot,' Dani said. 'Right on the mark.'

He straightened up, and turned to her. He dropped the shell into a pocket. 'Like I said, the pits.'

He handed the shotgun to Bruce, the prop master.

'You did fine,' Dani told him. She took his arm, and led him off to the side.

'Sorry I screwed up,' he said.

'Roger's a bastard.'

'No, he was right. I screwed up.'

'That's no reason for him to fly off the handle. He's a spoiled baby.'

Jack pulled the ski mask off his head, and rubbed his face. Stroking his ruffled beard, he shook his head. 'I am sorry. It made you look bad.'

'Hey, we're doing great work for that turkey. Our efforts are the only saving grace in his stupid, hare-brained movie, and he'd better realise it.'

Jack appeared, for an instant, as if he might laugh. Then his face darkened. He gnawed his lower lip, and looked into Dani's eyes. 'That first time, when I was taking aim . . . Hell, you'll think I'm crazy, but I got the feeling it was you in the window. Really *you*. A switch got pulled, or something. I just couldn't shoot. I had to make sure . . . and then I saw you standing over there with Michael, and I was all right.'

Dani stared at Jack. She remembered the day, only two months ago, when he had entered her house for the job interview. His size and shaggy beard had intimidated her, at first; he looked like a wild mountain man. But his mild, intelligent eyes and quiet voice quickly won her over. She liked him, hired him over thirty-two other applicants who's responded to her ad in the *Reporter*. He soon proved himself to be a competent employee – better than competent: energetic and eager, a fast learner, innovative and usually cheerful. But he'd been an employee, nothing more. They'd kept their emotional distance, stayed safely impersonal.

Until now.

Looking into his eyes, Dani felt a warm tremor of excitement.

'Guess it's out of the bag,' he said, a worried, glad look on his face.

'I guess so,' Dani said. 'What'll we do about it?'

'How about a kiss?'

She stepped close to Jack, felt his arms wrap around her, pull her snugly against his parka. Hugging him, she tipped back her head. He smiled down at her. His lips and beard pressed her mouth.

She knew that others might be watching, but she didn't care. It only mattered that this man she had worked with, joked with, had wanted her all along and kept it to himself. If he hadn't hesitated to shoot Ingrid, the masquerade might have gone on and on .

She eased her mouth away. 'How come you never . . . said anything?'

'Didn't want to get canned. Look what happened to Al.'

She winced at the mention of her previous assistant. 'He was a turkey.'

'A turkey who put moves on you.'

'How'd you know that?'

'Just a guess. His work was good: he went straight from you to the Steinman Studios. So it had to be something else.'

'He tried to . . . 'Dani's face burned. 'He thought I was being coy when I told him to lay off. He tried to force the issue.'

'Bastard.'

'Well, it's over. He got canned and you got the job, so it all worked out for the best.'

'Indeed it did,' Jack said.

Dani grinned at him. 'Indeed, indeed.'

# THREE

'To INGRID,' Dani toasted.

'May she rest in peace.'

Dani clinked the rim of her vodka and tonic against Jack's, and took a sip. They were sitting outside at Joe Allen, the restaurant where she'd been fêted several months ago by Roger and the producer of *Midnight Screams*. She remembered listening to their eager descriptions of the effects they envisioned and finally, over coffee, signing the contract. The contract led to Ingrid, to Jack's revelation. It seemed only fitting that she should bring Jack here tonight.

A starting place, of sorts.

She stared at him, nervous and excited, wondering if he felt the same way. He certainly didn't look nervous. Puzzled, maybe, studying her eyes as if searching for answers to the same questions that whirled through Dani's own mind: where will this lead, to joy and fulfillment and an end to the loneliness, or to a bitter parting? The alternatives seemed too big, the chances of failure too great. She suddenly felt overwhelmed and afraid. She set down her glass. It left her hand cold and wet. She rubbed her hands together, squeezed them, pressed them to her chin.

'Dani?'

She tried to smile. 'I'm not sure if I'm ready for this.'

'Me too. Let's forget the whole thing.'

His response shocked her into laughter. 'You creep!'

'See how easy it is, now that we don't have to worry about a serious relationship, a commitment, the heartache of rejection?'

'Much easier,' she admitted. 'But I think I prefer it the other way.'

'I do, too.'

'We'll give it a try.'

'At least till something better comes along.'

'You *are* a creep!'

'See?' Jack said. 'You're already starting to plumb the depths of my being.'

The waiter came and they both ordered ribs. When the meal came, Jack said, 'Be messy. Don't make me look bad.' Dani found that she didn't have to try. The juices and tangy sauce clung to her fingers, trickled down her chin. Fortunately, the table was well stocked with napkins. She used plenty, but Jack used more. She watched him, amused, as he swiped at his dripping mustache and beard.

'You should feel honored,' he said. 'I wouldn't humiliate myself, this way, in front of just anyone.'

'You look like a bear in a honey jar.'

'Please. It's hard enough to maintain dignity eating bones without comparisons to Gentle Ben.'

'I was thinking of Winnie the Pooh.'

'Gasp. Groan. How *could* you?'

When the stripped bones lay heaped on their plates, Jack said, 'I'm gonna need soap and water. Back in a minute.'

He left. Settling back in her chair, Dani looked around the restaurant. She saw waiters hurrying to crowded tables. She saw men gesturing at each other with forks, a late arrival greeting his companion with a shoulder slap, a hollow-cheeked beauty sipping wine at the table two older men who talked vigorously and ignored her, a slick young man with an open shirt and gold necklaces, holding the hand of a girl who looked sixteen and awe-struck.

The man seemed too earnest, a sure sign that he was handing out a line. The girl looked innocent. She would buy the line, whatever it might be, and probably live to regret it. She would lose some of that youth, that innocence. Next time around, she would be more cautious.

But not too cautious, Dani hoped. You've got to take chances.

Her stomach fluttered. Jack would be returning any minute. Dinner was nearly over. Then they would drive to her house, if only because Jack's car was parked there. A great relief to just kiss him goodnight at the door, postpone the tense, wonderful time of intimacy. Perhaps they would both be better off waiting.

But she knew it wouldn't happen that way. Now that she'd found him, discovered the truth, she wanted him too much.

They would go to her house and make love.

She reached for her wine. The surface of the Sauvignon Blanc shimmered as she lifted the glass to her lips.

'Danielle Larson?'

Startled, she jerked her head to the right. A man on the sidewalk waved. Dani stared, trying to recognise him: tall, so skinny he looked as if his black turtleneck was all that held his bones together, hairless and pale. With his back to the lights of the street, however, shadows concealed the features of his face.

He looked like no-one Dani knew, or wanted to know.

But he'd called her name. She didn't want to snub him, so she waved.

He began to run toward her. Dani caught her breath. Goosebumps stiffened her skin. This is a put-on, she told herself. Nobody runs like that, on tiptoes, hunched over, arms up like a goddamn boogyman ready to grab a throat.

It's a joke.

But he was plunging straight for the patio railing, straight for Dani.

Someone screamed.

Dani shot her chair back and leaped away. Her shoulder caught a passing man. He started to fall. Their feet tangled and Dani dropped onto him. 'Geez. I'm sorry, I'm sorry,' she muttered, scurrying off.

'Quite all right. Any time.'

She looked toward the railing. No sign of the intruder. But a crowd had gathered there as if everyone in the restaurant had raced over for a look at the phantom. They talked in a rush.

'Some kind of nut.'

'Run, you bastard!' a man yelled.

'Matters are coming to a pretty pass when one . . . '

'Probably freaked out on Angel Dust.'

'Certainly sparked things up.'

'Where's the manager?'

As the commentary continued, Dani pushed herself to her feet. Her skirt was twisted awry, her green silk blouse untucked. She was trying to straighten herself when Jack came out. His mouth dropped open. She saw alarm on his face. It changed to relief when he spotted her. He eased his way through the throng of guests returning to their tables.

Then he reached Dani and took hold of her shoulders. 'You all right?'

'I'm okay. Just a bit rumpled.'

'What *happened*?'

She shrugged. 'I'm not really sure. Some guy on the sidewalk called my name and waved. Next thing I knew, he was running for the patio like a madman.'

Jack frowned. 'Did he say anything?'

'I didn't stick around to find out.'

'But he was coming for you?'

'Sure looked that way.'

'Let's get the hell out of here.'

Against Dani's protests, Jack paid the bill. On the sidewalk in front of the restaurant, she kissed him. 'Thank you for the dinner. It was supposed to be my treat, you know.'

'I'm a chauvinist.'

'I'd better raise your salary.'

'Feel free.'

He took her hand and they headed for her car. Dani wished she hadn't parked so far away. During her eight years in Los Angeles, she'd developed the habit of taking the first parking place within walking range of her goal. It saved her from crowded, expensive parking lots, from the intimidation of valet parking, from circling blocks in a frustrating search for an empty stretch of curb. Sometimes, the practice backfired. She would walk three blocks only to discover a parking space directly in front of her destination. Tonight, she wondered if the strange, skinny man might be lurking nearby, ready to spring out at them. The sanctuary of the car remained a block away, around the corner on Robertson Blvd.

She held Jack's hand more tightly.

'It's all right,' he said.

25

'I hope so.'

'Do you have *any* idea who it might've been?'

'Not the slightest.'

'But he knew you. Did you tell anyone you'd be here tonight?'

'Nobody,' she said, and heard the quiet tread of footsteps from the rear.

They both looked back. The lone man, far behind them, waddled along in a pale suit and Stetson, a cigar poking from his mouth.

'That him?'

Dani smiled with relief. 'Not unless he's a were-oaf.'

'A *were*–oaf?'

'By day, a cadaverous vegetarian. But when the full moon rises, a strange sensation grips his body. He pulses with throbbing corpulence. His clothes burst at the strain and he sags out, four hundred pounds of shimmering obesity, driven by an insatiable need to stalk the night in search of lasagne.'

'Wow,' Jack said, 'you oughta run that by Roger.'

'Yeah, he'd probably go for it. He went for *Midnight Screams*, didn't he? Call it *An American Were-oaf in Sardi's*.'

'Or *The Slobbering*.'

They rounded the corner, laughing, and Dani spotted her white VW Rabbit halfway up the block. She started to walk faster. Freeing her hand from Jack's, she reached into her purse for the keys.

Across the street, the brake lights of a car glared red. The car stopped.

'Oh boy,' Dani muttered.

'Hope it's not stopping for us,' Jack said.

The car was a black hearse. It didn't move.

'Maybe he needs directions to Forest Lawn.'

'Funny,' Dani said.

The hearse began to creep along, keeping pace with them as they hurried to the Rabbit.

'Want me to check?' Jack asked.

'No!'

Dani rushed into the street and unlocked her door. She climbed in, jerked it shut, and locked it. Then she leaned across the passenger seat to unlock Jack's side. As he lowered himself into the car, the hearse sped away.

Dani twisted around to watch it. At the end of the block, it turned onto a sidestreet. 'Well, it's gone.'

'For now,' Jack said.

'Bite your tongue.' She started her car and pulled away from the curb, keeping her eyes on the rearview mirror. The road behind her was clear for a moment. Then headlights pushed into the intersection. The long, dark body of a car swung onto the road. 'Oh shit,' Dani muttered.

Jack looked around. 'Is it the hearse?'

'I couldn't tell for sure. I think so.'

'Well, don't worry.'

'Tell that to my stomach.'

'Don't worry, stomach.'

With a nervous laugh, she flicked her turn signal on. At least the traffic light was green; she wouldn't have to stop and let the car catch up and find out, for sure, that it was the hearse.

She made her turn, and the car vanished from her mirror. Speeding up Third Street, she continued to watch. The traffic light changed, and a line of waiting cars started through the intersection. Dani sighed as if given a reprieve. 'That should hold him,' she said.

'It probably wasn't the hearse, anyway. And if it was, there's still no reason to think it's following us.'

As they passed Joe Allen, Dani's eyes moved from the lighted, bustling patio to the deserted sidewalk where the stranger had called to her.

Her scalp suddenly prickled. 'It's him,' she whispered.

'What?'

'It's him! I know it. The guy in the hearse, it's the one who ran at me. He hung around, followed us to the car.'

'No. Come on.'

'Yes!'

'Come on, this isn't one of Roger's splatter movies, it's real life.'

'I don't care.'

'It does make a difference, Dani. If we were characters in some

27

damn thriller, I'd say sure, the nut hopped into his hearse, he's gonna follow us and treat us to a nasty death – special make-up effects by Danielle Larson.'

In the rearview mirror, the stream of cars was drawing closer.

'But this is real life. The nut was probably just a harmless space case. The guy in the hearse probably just stopped on the road to get his bearings, figured out his mistake, and turned around to get on the right track. Two unrelated incidents.'

'I hope you're right,' Dani said.

'So do I,' Jack looked over his shoulder. 'There it is,' he said without excitement.

'Where?'

'Second car back, in the other lane.'

'What should I do?'

'Just keep going,' Jack said, and faced the front.

'Toward home?'

'He'll probably turn off. Chances are that he's *not* following us. Really. I can think of several times I was absolutely convinced cars were tailing me. They stayed back there, turn after turn. But nothing ever came of it. They just happened to be heading the same way.'

'Yeah, I've gone through that too.' She eased into the left-hand turn lane.

Jack looked around.

'Is it there?'

'Afraid so. Just behind this Mercedes.'

'Oh Jack.'

'Everybody takes Crescent Heights from here.'

Dani knew he was right. The road led directly into Laurel Canyon Boulevard, one of the few routes over the hills to the western side of the valley. The knowledge, however, didn't ease her mind.

'When do we decide he *is* following us?' she asked. 'Our next turn-off's Asher. By then, it'll be too late.'

The signal changed, and she made her left turn.

Jack was silent for a few moments. Then he said, 'I think we'd better play it safe. We certainly don't want to lead him to your door.'

'That's for sure.'

'What's the road before Asher?'

'Dona Lola.'

'Okay, take that instead. If he turns there, we'll know.'

'Then what?'

'We'll worry about that when it happens.'

'Don't you mean *if* it happens?'

'Right, if.'

They continued up Crescent Heights. Though Dani kept checking the rearview, there was always at least one car between them and the hearse. Jack, sitting sideways, had a better view and sometimes spotted it.

'We're coming up on Sunset,' Dani finally said. She drove this route almost every day. Half the cars, she knew, would turn off at Sunset – a major boulevard and the last opportunity to leave Crescent Heights before it became Laurel Canyon and climbed into the hills.

She drove through the intersection. 'Is it . . . ?'

'Still with us.'

'Oh shit.' She wiped her sweaty hands on her skirts.

'Just means he's heading toward the valley like the rest of us.'

'Yeah.'

The narrow road led upward, twisting and banking, the darkness of the wooded hillsides unbroken except for an occasional window light.

'Isn't that store up ahead?' Jack asked. 'That old-fashioned country store?'

Dani nodded.

'Pull into its parking lot. But do it suddenly, if you can, and don't signal.'

'What if *he* pulls in?'

'At least there should be some people around.'

'Okay,' Dani said. She didn't want to do it, wished she had more time to prepare herself. Dona Lola was five minutes away, but seemed like the distant future compared to this.

The road curved and she saw the well-lighted store standing among the trees. A man with a grocery bag was climbing down its wooden stairs. Half a dozen cars were parked in its lot.

Jack was right. A good place to confront the hearse. Certainly better than the lonely darkness of Dona Lola Drive.

She checked the mirror. The car behind her was a safe distance back. Suddenly, she jerked the steering wheel to the right. They hurtled into the parking lot and she hit the brakes.

Twisting around, she gazed back at the cars on Laurel Canyon. The hearse sped by, along with the others.

Dani slumped back in her seat and sighed. She felt exhausted.

For a few moments, they sat in silence. Then Jack said, 'Would you like me to drive the rest of the way?'

'No, it's all right. We're almost there.' She turned the car around, waited for a break in the traffic, then accelerated onto the road. 'Anybody ever tell you you're brilliant?'

'Only my mother.'

'Well, you are.'

Jack smiled. 'The guy probably wasn't following us, anyway.'

'Probably not,' Dani said. 'After all, this isn't one of Roger's splatter movies. This is real life. Hearses don't tail you in real life.'

'Right.'

'Right.'

She wanted to believe it, but couldn't. She doubted if Jack really believed it, either. She wasn't terribly surprised when, at the crest of the hill where Mulholland intersected Laurel Canyon, they came upon a black motionless shape on the road's shoulder.

The hearse.

It had waited for them.

It swung onto the road behind them.

Dani wasn't terribly surprised, but she wanted badly to scream.

# FOUR

SHE SWUNG onto Dona Lola. The hearse followed. 'Now what?'

'Stop the car,' Jack said.

'Here?' The street was dark and deserted. A few cars were parked along the curbs, and light shone in the windows of nearby houses, but nobody moved about.

'Let's see what he does.'

With a nod, Dani slowed the car, stopped it. She shifted to neutral and set the emergency brake.

In the rearview mirror, she watched the hearse creep closer. A few yards behind them, it stopped. The driver was alone. His face was a dim blur, craters of darkness where his eyes should be. His head was hairless.

'It's him,' Dani whispered. 'The guy from the restaurant.'

Jack looked through the back window. 'Are you sure?'

'I think so.'

The high beams of the hearse went on, shooting light into the car. It glared off the mirror. Squinting against the painful brightness, Dani shoved the mirror. It tipped upward, shining at the ceiling.

Jack faced the front. 'Obnoxious s.o.b.'

'What does he want?'

'Obviously, he wants to scare you.'

'At least,' Dani muttered.

'You know, it might be a practical joke. Maybe someone hired this guy to throw a little fun into your life.'

'It's a *prank*?'

'I wouldn't rule it out. After all, look at the irony of it: the queen of horror effects pursued through the night by a creep in a hearse.'

Dani nodded. 'It *could* be someone's idea of a joke.'

'Someone with a rather cruel and tasteless sense of humor.'

'Michael?'

'What about your old friend, Al?'

'My God, do you know what film he's on now? *The Under-taker.*'

Jack whistled. 'I believe the mystery is solved.'

'Not quite. How did he know we'd be at Joe Allen tonight?'

'Could've followed us from the studio. He'd recognise your car, wouldn't he?'

'Sure.'

'The weirdo didn't show up till we were done eating. Al probably phoned, let him know where to find us, and the guy hustled on over.'

'Al's certainly capable of it,' Dani said. 'I wouldn't put it past him, but . . . I don't know.'

'It's the only solution that makes sense.'

'Don't!' she cried as Jack pushed open the door.

'I'll be right back.'

'Jack, for Godsake!'

He flung the door shut and marched toward the hearse. Dani sprang from the car. She took a step toward the hearse, but fear hit her like an icy gale, forcing her backwards against the open door.

'Jack, come on!'

He tugged at the handle of the passenger door. The hearse rocked slightly.

Then the driver's door flew open. The man leaped out and ran at Dani, arms out, mouth agape.

His pointed teeth, she knew at once, were plastic vampire fangs.

*A gag. It's all a sick gag.*

Jack was charging past the front of the hearse, trying to head him off. But Dani saw that he wouldn't make it.

The lunging, cadaverous man was already too close, his demented murmur loud in Dani's ears.

She jumped into the car and slammed the door. As she pounded the lock button down, he grabbed the outside handle. He jerked it, shaking the car.

Then he pressed his young face to the window. He grinned like a madman, his nose and chin mashed against the pane, his eyes rolling. His tongue darted out between his plastic fangs and licked the glass.

Jack reached for him, but he jumped back, whirled around and ran.

Jack dashed after him. They sprinted up the street. The boy had given up his weird, hunched gate. He ran, now, with amazing speed, his head tucked down, his arms pumping, his legs whipping out in long, quick strides. The gap between him and Jack slowly widened. He cut to the right and raced up a lawn. As he vanished behind the corner of a dark house, Jack wheeled around and ran back.

Leaning across the seat, Dani opened the door for him.

But he didn't get in. He rushed by. Twisting around, Dani saw him crouch beside a front tire of the hearse. He removed something, flicked it away. The air cap? His hand shoved into a pocket and came out with a small object Dani couldn't see. He pressed it to the tire.

She looked toward the house, studied the darkness at both sides. The boy was nowhere to be seen.

She turned around. Jack still crouched by the tire.

'Hurry,' she whispered.

Then she realised that she could help. She shoved the shift into first, swung the car into a driveway on the left, and backed out.

She stopped beside the hearse.

Jack stood up. He stepped away from the flat tire and slipped his key case into his pocket. Then he climbed in beside Dani.

In the dome light, she saw speckles of sweat on his forehead. He grinned at her, looking both angry and gleeful. 'That'll fix the little asshole,' he said, and swung the door shut.

Dani sped toward the rushing headlights of traffic on Laurel Canyon.

# FIVE

DRIVING UP Asher Lane, Dani kept her eyes on the rearview mirror. Headlights pushed through the darkness on Laurel Canyon, but none swept onto the narrow road.

As a precaution, she killed her own headlights. The arc lamps along the lane were spaced far apart with dark gaps separating their pools of light, but they gave enough brightness to steer by.

'I think we're okay,' Jack said. 'Even if he had an air can, we got a big enough jump on him.'

'Hope so,' Dani muttered.

She pulled into her driveway and stopped beside Jack's Mustang. She turned off the engine. Leaning against the steering wheel, she let out a shaky sigh. Jack's hand stroked her back.

'It's all right now,' he said.

'Will you come in with me?'

'Sure.'

'I'm just . . . it really shook me up a bit.'

'I know. Me, too. But I'm sure . . . the guy was probably harmless, just doing what he was paid for. Al or Michael – whoever's behind this – probably dug him up at central casting.'

'Or Forest Lawn.'

Jack laughed softly. His big, warm hand continued to rub her back. 'I . . . '

Dani waited. 'What?'

'Well,' he sighed. 'I do think we've lost the guy, but we ought to play it safe.'

Dani raised her head off the backs of her hands and looked at him. His face was a pale smudge, his familiar features masked by darkness. Only the feel of his hand assured Dani that this was Jack and not a stranger.

'What do you mean?' she asked.

'He might . . . I don't think we should leave your car here.'

'Oh Jack,' she said.

'Maybe I'm over reacting, but we don't want this guy to find out where you live. If we leave it here, it's like a name tag.'

Her mind fought against the suggestion. Couldn't she even park in front of her own house? What about tomorrow and the next day? 'You could've gone all night without saying that.'

'I'm sorry.'

'He doesn't know which street we're on.'

'He's only one away.'

'Al knows my address. If he hired the guy . . . '

'What if he didn't?'

'Oh shit. Then who *is* he?'

Jack shook his head. 'Maybe we can get it into the garage.'

The garage was her workshop, crowded with shelves, a work-bench and tables, lamps and stools, all the tools of her craft and the make-up appliances she'd created for a dozen different films. She considered trying to clear a space. 'That'd take . . . no, forget it.'

'Let's park it up the street, then.'

'In front of somebody *else's* house?'

'Got any obnoxious neighbors?'

She surprised herself by laughing. 'That's wicked.' The laughter seemed to nudge her fear aside. When she finished, she found herself almost calm. 'Look, let's go inside. We'll leave the car here. If this kid's so goddamn determined to find my house, he'll manage it one way or another, anyhow. Sooner or later. I'm not, for Godsake, going to spend the rest of my life hiding from him.'

Jack squeezed her shoulder. 'Let's go in, then.'

They climbed from the car. As they walked over the cobble-stones toward the front door, Dani heard a car engine. Her knees went weak. Looking around, she saw a car gliding slowly up the street. It passed.

A pale Mercedes.

With a sigh, she hurried into the dark recess of the front stoop. Jack stood beside her as she unlocked the door. They stepped

35

into the lighted foyer. She shut the door and secured its guard chain.

Jack's hands curled over her shoulders. He turned her around, pulled her gently against him. She held him tightly. The strength of his body felt safe and comfortable.

'Thank God you were with me tonight,' she said. She tilted her head back, and they kissed. The pressure of his mouth soothed her. The tension eased out. She felt peaceful enough to fall asleep in his arms.

Then his mouth went away. 'I think it's time to call the police.'

'Oh no.'

'If the guy's still in the neighborhood, they might pick him up.'

'Yeah. All right.' Reluctantly, she let go of Jack. He kept hold of her hand, and they walked away from the door. The living room was lighted by a single lamp. The black expanse of its picture windows, at the rear, made her nervous. Leaving Jack, she hurried across the carpet to the draw cords. She kept her eyes down, unwilling to look at the window, afraid of what she might see in the darkness beyond. As she closed the curtains, she heard Jack dialing.

'Yes,' he said. 'We have a prowler . . . 822 Asher Lane . . . Laurel Canyon Boulevard . . . Okay, thanks.' He hung up

'A prowler?' Dani asked.

'Close enough.'

'How about a drink?' she asked, and turned on a lamp by the couch.

'Sounds good.'

She turned on another lamp while Jack walked down the long side of the L-shaped bar. He entered the kitchen and turned on a light. 'Ten twenty-five,' he said.

The doorbell rang at five to eleven, making Dani's hand jump. She set down her vodka and tonic.

'That was quick,' Jack said. 'Twenty minutes. Good thing we didn't *need* them.'

She followed Jack to the foyer. He slipped off the guard chain and opened the door. Two uniformed patrolmen were waiting on the front stoop. 'You reported a prowler?' asked the taller man. The other, an oriental, tapped his night-stick against the side of his leg and seemed to be staring at Dani's chin.

'That's right,' Jack said. 'He just took off, though. Two or three minutes ago. In a black hearse.'

'Did you get the license number?'

'Afraid not.'

'Can you describe the man?' he asked, raising a clipboard.

'A Caucasian, maybe eighteen or twenty, very thin, bald. He wore a black turtleneck and jeans.'

Without a word, the other patrolman strode away.

'Did he attempt an entry of the premises?'

Jack shook his head. 'He was around back, looking at the windows. Scared the hell out of us. I yelled at him, but he wouldn't leave. He stayed back there, walking around the pool and watching us. I wasn't about to go out. You know? I figured he might be dangerous. So I phoned you people. He finally ran off, and we saw him get into the hearse.'

The patrolman nodded and glanced up from his clipboard. 'May I have your names?'

'I'm Jack Somers. This is Danielle Larson.'

'Whose residence is this?'

'Mine,' Dani said.

'All right.' He jabbed the pen into his shirt pocket. 'We'll see what we can do.'

'We appreciate it,' Jack said.

'Yes. Thank you.'

He aimed a forefinger at them, making a snicking sound against the side of his cheek, and winked. Then he turned away.

Jack shut the door.

'Good grief,' Dani said. 'What'd you do?'

'What, the fabrication?'

'You lied through your teeth. To the *police*!'

'I know. Naughty, huh?'

'Jack!'

'They'll never be the wiser unless they catch the guy.'

'Why not just tell the truth?'

'The truth was too complicated. A prowler's nice and simple –

and ominous. I figured it'd be more likely to catch the interest of the officers . . . *involve* them.'

'It'll certainly involve *us*, if they nab the guy.'

'They'll understand.'

'You're crazy.'

'Does that mean you don't like me any more?' His eyes widened slightly.

Dani gazed at him, suddenly feeling weak and shaky. 'Doesn't mean that,' she finally whispered. She stepped out of her shoes, moved forward and began to open the buttons of his plaid shirt.

'Guess not,' he said.

Her fingers trembled. Her mouth was dry. She was surprised to be taking the lead this way. She didn't understand it, but she couldn't stop herself. She spread open Jack's shirt, pulling sharply to untuck its front, then let her hands glide over the smooth warm skin of his belly, the soft mat of chest hair. She lingered over the firm mounds of his pectorals. Leaning forward, she found a nipple with her tongue.

Jack moaned. He pulled her blouse from her skirt, and she felt his touch on the bare skin of her back, bunching up the blouse as they moved higher. Its silken front crept up her belly, taut and rubbing. Its folds seemed to trap her breasts for a moment. Then it flipped over them, releasing them.

She eased her face away from Jack's chest, and raised her arms. For a moment, their eyes met. Jack looked like a boy, full of hope and excitement but worried that he might somehow lose out. Then his face vanished behind a translucent curtain of green. The curtain lifted, tickling Dani's back and breasts, sliding up her arms. She saw Jack's belly, his bushy chest, his beard and gleaming eyes.

He flung her blouse aside and gazed at her. 'You're beautiful,' he whispered. He touched her shoulders. His fingers trembled over her collar bones, down her chest. They traced the outlines of her breasts.

She sucked a deep, shaky breath, arching her back as his thumbs grazed her nipples.

She opened her skirt. It dropped to her feet and she stood before Jack naked except for her panties. Crouching, he kissed a nipple. He licked it, took it between his lips. Dani clenched his long hair, gasping as he sucked her nipple, as he slipped her panties down, as a hand eased upward between her thighs. It pushed against her. Every muscle flinched rigid. A ragged groan escaped her throat.

She forced Jack's head away, bent over and kissed him. She thrust her tongue into his mouth, shuddering as his fingers slipped into her.

Her legs trembled. She fell to her knees, Jack staying with her. In a frenzy, she tugged open his belt, unbuttoned the waist of his trousers, jerked his zipper down. His trim belly sucked in as she clawed at the band of his shorts. She pulled the band toward her. The shiny head of his erection sprang out. In a fever, she tugged his pants to his knees. Her fingers encircled him, slid down, feeling the heat and thickness of his shaft.

Jack's hand went away. It was slick on her back as he lowered her to the soft nap of the carpet. He braced himself above her, his open shirt hanging down, caressing her sides. She stroked his back. Her fingers dug in as she felt the touch of his penis. Then he was lower, pushing gently, easing into her, sliding in deeper and deeper.

Her fingers relaxed and she sighed, savoring the fullness. She felt possessed, as if the penis had penetrated her hidden center and made her somehow a part of Jack. Raising her knees high, she felt it move farther into her. She worked muscles, tightening herself around the shaft, wanting it to stay forever.

It withdrew, but only to push in again. And then it was thrusting, sliding almost out, plunging as if in need of a deeper connection, jolting her body as it rammed.

Jack lowered himself. His chest mashed her breasts. His mouth covered hers. His tongue shoved it. Dani felt it thick and wet in her mouth, probing while his erection filled her below.

It was suddenly too much. She jerked taut, gasping, and as her body quaked with release she felt Jack throb inside her, felt his spurting rush of semen.

He lay heavily on her as they both tried to catch their breath. When he tried to raise himself, Dani hugged him tightly and wrapped her legs around him. 'Stay,' she whispered.

'Don't want to crush you.'

'It's fine.' She lay motionless, comfortable beneath his weight, feeling him still inside her where he belonged like a part of her own body.

She felt incomplete when he finally withdrew, but his presence remained like a warm imprint and she still held his fluid like a gift left behind.

She sat up carefully. It rolled inside her. It trickled down her thighs as she hurried to the bathroom.

The rest of the house was dark when she stepped out. She stood near the door, staring down the corridor. Fear crawled up her back.

'Jack?'

A pale figure appeared near the foyer.

'Is that you?'

'I hope so.'

'Did you turn the lights out?'

'Do you want them back on?'

'No. It just . . . gave me a little scare.'

He came up the dark corridor, and Dani was pleased to find him still naked. She raised her arms. He stepped into them and pulled her gently against her body. His hands glided down her back, held her buttocks.

'Will you stay the night?'

'If you want.'

'I want.'

'Good.'

She turned off the bathroom light. Taking Jack's hand, she led him to her bedroom. Its curtains were open, letting moonlight in through the sliding glass door.

'I'll close that,' she said.

They crossed the room. She started to pull her hand away, but Jack kept his grip. 'Let me look at you in the moonlight,' he whispered.

Dani nodded. They stepped close to the glass and faced one another. Though all she could see of Jack's eyes were glinting specks, she felt his gaze like a soft caress. Her skin tingled. Her nipples rose erect. A warm rush surged through her.

She studied Jack. Naked in the moonlight, he looked like a

bearded giant. His shoulders were broad, his arms and chest bulging with muscle, his belly lean. He stood with his sturdy legs slightly spread. His dark sac hung between them. His penis was pale and rising.

'You're quite a hunk,' she said.

His laughter burst out. He lunged at Dani, grabbed her arms and swung her toward the bed. The mattress caught her behind the knees, and she sprawled backwards, laughing. She yelped as he nibbled her thigh. Then they both were rolling on the bed. Straddling him, she pinned his arms down. He raised his head, licked her breast. No longer laughing, she relinquished her hold on his wrists and scooted down, rubbing his chest. She flinched with the shock of desire as her anus rammed the blunt stake of his erection. She raised herself, felt it slide along her other opening, and drove backwards, gasping as she impaled herself.

She pressed her face against Jack's chest. She nuzzled the matted hair with her cheek, listening to the thunder of his heart, and suddenly she felt her insides shrivel.

A dark figure was pressed against the glass door, staring in. *Him*!

His fingers clawed the glass.

'Jack,' she whispered.

She scurried free, rolled aside, and Jack sprang for the door. Sitting up, she saw that the intruder had already vanished. Jack tugged the door. With a low curse, he clacked open its latch. Then he jerked it again. This time, it rumbled open. He stepped outside and looked both ways.

Dani raced forward. She stopped at the open door.

'Gone,' Jack said.

'Come back in. There's no point chasing him.'

'Fuckin' maniac.'

She stepped out, shivering as the cool night air wrapped her body, and placed a hand on Jack's shoulder. 'Come on.'

He suddenly flinched.

'What?'

Raising an arm, he pointed toward the swimming pool. The black rippling water was dappled with bright specks of moonlight. 'I don't . . . ' Her guts knotted. 'What *is* it?'

'I don't know. Maybe you'd better go inside.'

She shook her head and crossed her arms over the gooseflesh of her breasts.

Together, they walked alongside the pool toward the deep end and the *thing* on the diving board.

They reached the corner.

'A paper bag?' Jack whispered.

'But what's in it?'

'Wait here,' Jack said.

Dani waited, shivering. She pressed her palms to her rigid nipples and closed her legs tightly against a need to urinate.

Jack hesitated at the foot of the diving board. He turned around, scanning the darkness. Then he climbed up. He walked out over the water, the board vibrating slightly. Then he crouched down. He picked up the bag. The weight inside made its paper pull and crackle.

Holding it away from his body, Jack unfolded the top. He peered in.

'What is it?' Dani whispered.

'Can't see.'

He reached inside.

'Don't!'

He gasped and his hand darted out. For a moment, he seemed to lose his balance. He waved an arm through the air, steadied himself, then reached again into the bag.

This time, he brought it out clenching a fistful of hair. At the end of the hair dangled a human head. Its face turned, as if by intention, toward Dani. She stared at its bulging eyes, its gaping mouth and lolling tongue.

Dani realised she'd been holding her breath. She let it out quickly and sucked in the fresh, night air. 'If you tell me it's real, I'll scream.'

# SIX

LINDA ROLLED on her bed and gazed at the luminous face of her alarm clock. One thirty-six. The minute hand crept toward the next dot. She planned to wait until two, but time seemed to pass so terribly slowly.

She turned onto her back and stared at the ceiling. Her heart pounded fast. She rubbed her sweaty hands on her nightgown. Beneath them, her belly throbbed as if her entire body was pulsing with the frenzied heartbeat.

The surging blood made her left leg ache, and once again she saw herself lunging into the street, sobbing, blind with tears but almost home, and suddenly caught in a glare of headlights. Brakes screamed. She felt the impact, the blasting pain, saw herself tumble over the hood as if in slow motion, and remembered wondering in the eternal instant before she hit the windshield if this was bad enough to kill her and would it qualify as murder?

In her mind, it qualified. She'd been murdered by Tony and Arnold and Joel and the horrible maniac in the Freeman house, and nobody would ever know.

Let me be a ghost, she thought, so I can get them.

And then she had smacked through the windshield.

She awoke from her coma thin and weak, with a throbbing head and a leg in traction. Her parents acted as if she had, indeed, returned from the dead. While they wept, the doctor questioned her. Did she remember her name, her address, her birthday? Her parents looked tense until she gave the answers. Did she remember the night of the accident? Oh yes, she remembered it all. But a new, sly corner of her mind whispered not to tell.

I was walking home from the library, and then . . . and then . . . I don't know.

Perfectly normal with a trauma of this nature, the doctor assured everyone. Nothing to be concerned about. The mind's way of protecting itself.

The memory of her deceit thrilled her, pushed aside her fear, and she grinned at the ceiling.

She'd known, even then, what her mission would be. Her secret mission.

She glanced at the clock. Only three minutes had passed.

Folding her hands behind her head, she felt the soft brush of her hair. Her stomach knotted.

Don't you think about that.

She sat up quickly. No more thinking, no more waiting.

She swung her legs off the bed and carefully stood up. Though her left leg felt weak and achy, she knew it was strong enough. The cast had been off for two weeks. She'd exercised constantly to strengthen the slack muscles, and finally, today, decided she was ready.

She stepped to the open window and slipped her nightgown off. The warm night breathed against her, fragrant with summer, making her shiver with fearful delight. Her own breath trembled as she gazed from her high window. All the houses but one were dark. Nothing moved on the lawns, the sidewalks, the street. The neighborhood looked deserted as if everyone had fled a terrible menace.

Linda turned away from the window. Easing open a dresser drawer, she took out her Yankee ballcap and put it on. Only then did she allow herself to look in the mirror. She grinned, her teeth pale in the dim reflections. Taking out an Ace bandage, she wrapped her chest. The elastic band was only long enough to circle her body once, but she pulled it tight, squeezing her breasts until they hurt. She fastened the bandage in place with its tiny clips, then took a dark, plaid shirt from the drawer. Her brother's shirt, filched that day from the back of his closet. She put it on and closed the buttons. Rolling the sleeves up her forearms, she studied her image. In the large, loose shirt, her flattened breasts made only the slightest bulges. At a distance, anyone would think she was a boy.

44

From her closet, she took blue jeans and her Adidas running shoes. She slipped into them, and returned to the dresser.

She reached into the open drawer, pushed aside a neat stack of panties, and pulled out her father's .38 caliber Smith and Wesson revolver. Sucking in her belly, she pushed its barrel under the waistband of her jeans. The weapon felt big and cool. Its muzzle, tight against her groin, rubbed her as she stepped toward the door. She thought of moving it, but the sensation was hot and exciting.

She inched the door open. Leaning out, she glanced both ways. The hallway was empty and dark, no stripes of light showing beneath any of the doors.

She took long strides down the carpeted hall, silently rolling her feet from heel to toe just as she'd done that other night when three boys took her . . .

No, she couldn't let herself think about that.

In front of her brother's door, a floorboard groaned. She winced but kept walking, reminding herself that Bob slept like the dead.

She reached the head of the stairway and started down, one hand on the banister, shifting her weight to it whenever a step threatened to squeak. When she reached the bottom, she breathed more easily. Down here, small noises would mean nothing.

She hurried into the kitchen. From a large brandy snifter on top of the refrigerator she took two books of matches. She slipped them into her shirt pocket and headed for the connecting door to the garage.

The garage, with its single small window on the far side, was much darker than she'd expected. She bumped against her father's Imperial. Feeling along its side, she found the door handle. She pulled. The door opened, triggering the car's interior light.

Enough to see by. She found the empty milk carton on the cluttered shelf where she'd left it.

In front of the car, she stopped at the power mower. Crouching, she reached over it and picked up the tin of gasoline. Its weight overbalanced her. She stumbled, the gun barrel digging in painfully, her knee ramming the top of the mower. But she caught herself without dropping either the can or the milk carton. She straightened up. There was a warm pain, and she wondered if the gunsight had cut her. She nudged the pistol butt with her wrist, felt the barrel move away from the tender place. Then she stepped to the clear area beside the car.

She filled the milk carton, the gas fumes scorching her nostrils, bringing tears to her eyes. She returned the can, wondering if Bob would notice the missing fuel when he mowed the lawn next Saturday. Probably not. The two-gallon tin hadn't been completely full, and plenty of gas remained for filling the mower's small tank.

She picked up the milk carton. She pushed the car door shut, killing the light. Then she made her way through the darkness, one hand trailing along the car as a guide. She passed its rear, stepped across a gap to the trunk of her mother's Omni, felt her way up its far side, past the window, and found the garage's back door.

The night outside seemed almost bright, and cooler than the stuffy garage. Staying close to the shrubbery, she rushed across the yard to the gate. Its hinges squeaked, but in moments she was beyond it and striding down the alley.

Loose gravel crunched and scratched along the asphalt under her feet. A few nightbirds twittered, crickets sawed. Electricity hummed from the lines overhead. Linda listened for voices, for cars, for shutting doors or footsteps, ready to duck out of sight at the first hint of approach. But she heard none.

She began to wish for a human sound – even the far-off tinny voice from a television – or anything to assure her that someone, at least, remained awake, alive.

Nothing.

She walked alone in the night, vulnerable from every side, peering at the dark recesses behind garbage cans and telephone poles, between garages, often casting a glance over her shoulder.

At the end of the block, she looked up and down the street. Deserted. This is how I want it, she told herself, and hurried across. No people around, no witnesses. But her feeling of isolation grew like a hollowness inside as she entered the alley.

She thought about turning back.

No. She'd wanted this night since she first came out of the coma. Even before that, even while her broken body hurtled toward the windshield of the shrieking car. Wanted it, waited for it, prepared for it. Tonight was just the beginning. She couldn't quit now. Couldn't quit until she'd finished it all.

A rattling, metal noise startled Linda from her thoughts. She froze, gazing into the darkness ahead. Far down the alley, a dark shape broke away from the shadows and moved towards her. Linda's heart thundered like a fist trying to smash out of her chest. Gasping for breath, she squinted at the approaching shape.

What *is* it?

The clinking, rumbling sound grew louder as it moved. Then it entered a spill of moonlight and Linda saw a hunched figure shambling along behind a shopping cart.

She jerked the pistol free so it wouldn't hurt her, then whirled around and raced from the alley. She sprinted up the sidewalk. At a lighted street corner, she stopped to catch her breath, and looked back.

No sign of the weirdo with the shopping cart.

She pushed the pistol into her jeans and started walking. Though the street was deserted, it seemed less forbidding than the alleys. She felt as if she'd stumbled onto humanity after a detour into a strange, desolate land. The parked cars, the streetlamps, the rare lighted porches and house windows gave her comfort.

Once, a car turned onto the road. She pressed herself tightly to the trunk of an oak until it passed.

Though she walked for blocks, no other cars appeared. She saw a three-legged dog hobble along, glance at her without much interest, and urinate on a tree with a twist of its rump as if lifting the lost leg.

She saw a few fireflies glowing and vanishing. She saw a cat dash across the street and vanish beneath a parked station wagon. And then she was in front of the Benson house.

FOR SALE BY OWNER.

After tonight, Linda thought, maybe someone will dare to buy the place.

*We heard strange sounds at night,* Sheila had once told her.

Like women crying.

In the Freeman house?

And laughter. Real creepy laughter. The police came out, but they never found anyone.

Ghosts?

Don't laugh.

I don't believe in ghosts.

I do. Now I do.

Linda stepped past the hedge and saw the Freeman house. Fear crept up her spine, prickled the back of her neck. For a moment, she was in darkness, roped to the banister, the bony, naked man staring down at her. She clutched the milk carton to her chest, the gasoline sloshing inside.

Don't wait. Don't think about it.

She hurried up the sidewalk to the gate of the low picket fence. Turning around for a final check, she saw nobody. She opened the gate and rushed toward the house. The wooden stairs moaned under her weight. The blackness of the porch engulfed her.

Her hand found the door handle – cold as if the house's inner chill had passed through it. She pressed the upper plate. It sank. The tongue snapped back. With a slight push, the door started to open. It stopped abruptly with a shake of metal, and Linda saw the dim outline of a padlock just above her head.

Someone, probably the realtor, had come by since the night she was here, secured the front door.

She yanked the lock, twisted it, determined that it was securely latched. Her fingertips explored the mounting. Six screws held it in place, three in the doorframe and three in the door itself.

She pulled the pistol from her jeans. She slipped its barrel through the hoop of the lock hasp, and was about to tug when she realised that using it like a crowbar would mar the finish. Her father would know someone had used it. So she freed the barrel. She pushed it into her jeans again, glad to feel the return of its hard warm pressure.

Leaving the porch, she hoped for a moment that she wouldn't find a way into the house.

No, she *had* to get inside.

Burn the heart of it.

Burn the stairway.

She ran alongside the house, keeping close to the wall.

Burn the stairway. Let the flames trap *him* upstairs, if he's still lurking there. Let them wrap his hideous flesh, make it blister and snap, boil his eyes.

She raced up three stairs to the back door. There was no padlock. Its four windows shone in the moonlight. She rammed the gun muzzle through the pane on the lower right. As she reached through the hole, groping for the inside knob, her hip nudged the door open.

Not locked at all! Not even firmly shut.

She withdrew her arm, pushed the door wide, and stepped into the kitchen. Bits of glass crunched under her shoes. She halted, listening, then realised *he* might've heard the shattering panel, might even now be rising stiffly, reaching for his ax.

She hurried through the empty kitchen, down a passageway as chill and black as a cave, her ears keen for a sound from above. The stairway slanted down to her left. She sidestepped, peering up through the bars of its railing. Saw no-one. Rounding the newel post, she stared into the darkness at the top of the stairs where she'd first seen his pale shape standing motionless.

Linda pried open the carton. Holding her breath against the fumes, she began to splash gasoline on the lower stairs.

Somewhere above her, a floorboard creaked.

The quiet sound knocked her breath out. Numb with fear, she raised her eyes.

A dim shape seemed to grow from the top of the upper newel post.

A face.

Linda clamped her jaw tight to hold her scream inside. She swung out the carton, gas splattering the stairs.

The word 'No' floated down to her like a moan. Then the pale figure was lunging around the post. She flung the empty carton down. Clawing into her shirt pocket, she found her matches. She tore one free. The man was halfway down the stairs when it burst to life. She held its flame to the dark rows of match-heads. They flared, and she tossed the blazing pack at the stairs.

The gasoline erupted with a *whup* like a flag hit by a sudden gust. The fire reached up the man's naked body. Screaming, he shielded his face and staggered back. He twisted away from the fire, fell, and scurried up the stairs shrieking, slapping his blazing hair. He vanished into the corridor, and another scream mingled with his own – the high, piercing screech of a woman.

Confusion rolled through Linda's mind. She knew only that she had to get out. Covering her ears against the cries from above, she raced up the passageway to the kitchen, and outside.

She was a block away when the alarm began wailing to wake the volunteer firemen. She ducked into an alley, no longer afraid of the shambling creature with the shopping cart, no longer afraid of whatever else might lurk in the shadows.

She had burnt the Freeman house, burnt the naked specter that had haunted her nightmares.

It had to be him. He'd looked different, but it had to be him.

The woman's scream?

One of Sheila's ghosts?

No such thing. Nothing to be afraid of.

Not even the empty darkness of the alley. Nothing could touch her.

# SEVEN

DANI ROLLED over and opened one eye. Jack was missing. She smelled coffee, and smiled. Turning onto her belly, she pushed her face into the pillow and snuggled against the sheet.

There was no hurry. She wasn't needed at the studio today.

She writhed, stretching her stiff muscles, remembering how they got that way. Last night had been wonderful in spite of the creep.

Maybe she should thank the guy. He'd provided a certain excitement . . .

Excitement, my ass.

He'd scared the hell out of her. He ought to be caged, the damned degenerate.

She thought of him at the window, watching her with Jack, and her skin turned hot. The bed was no longer comfortable. She tossed aside the single sheet and climbed off. Taking her satin robe from the closet, she headed for the open door.

She found Jack at the bar, a coffee mug at his elbow, his fingers probing the mouth of the artificial head. He grinned around at her. 'Amateur night,' he said. Swiveling his stool, he rested the head on his lap. He flicked its red hair. 'Cheap wig. The eyes were marbles.' He pulled the tongue from its gaping mouth. 'A slab of liver.'

'Yuck.'

Jack flung it onto the counter. 'The guy has, at least, got a certain macabre ingenuity.'

He tossed the head to Dani. She inspected its waxy flesh, its eye sockets and mouth.

'Mortician's wax,' Jack said, 'on one of those plastic skulls you can buy at a hobby shop.'

51

Dani inserted her forefinger in an eye hole. It pushed against a soft, rubbery substance. She pulled it out, glanced at the gray crescent under her nail, sniffed it. 'Modeling clay.'

'To give it some weight, I suppose.'

'Well, Al obviously wasn't involved. No one with any knowledge of the business would turn out this kind of work.'

Jack raised a forefinger. 'Unless, Sherlock, he did it that way to throw off suspicion.'

'Or as a joke,' Dani added. She set the head down on the counter, and kissed Jack. 'Good moring.'

'Good morning,' he whispered. 'Excuse me if I don't touch.'

'Me too,' Dani picked up the slab of liver and eyed it critically. 'Not enough for both of us. Would you rather have bacon?'

'I think so.'

She carried the liver into the kitchen, holding her breath against the stench, and put it down the disposal. Then she washed her hands.

Jack washed up while she took the foil-wrapped bacon from the freezer. She unwrapped the rigid strips, dropped them into a skillet, and turned on a burner.

Jack came up behind her. He stroked her hair away, and she squirmed as he kissed the side of her neck. He rubbed her belly. A hand slipped inside her robe. It glided up her ribs, closed over her breast. His other hand loosened the cloth belt. He spread the robe open. He held both breasts, squeezing gently. Then his big hands moved lower, touching her skin like a warm breeze as they drifted down her ribs and belly. caressed her hips, brushed over her thighs. She quivered as the hands curved upward between her legs. They stirred her tuft of hair. She waited, but they didn't seek deeper.

Turning around, she embraced Jack and kissed his open mouth. He held her tightly. Then his arms loosened and Dani stepped back. She stood motionless while he closed her robe and adjusted the belt.

'You have a nice way of saying good morning,' she whispered.

'When my hands are clean.'

'Two eggs?'

He nodded.

'Will you stay?'

'Let's see how well you cook.'

'No, really. I . . . I mean, aside from just plain wanting you here, I . . . I guess I'm chicken. That guy worries me.'

'I'll stay. At least for a while. We'll see how it goes.'


Jack swabbed up the last of his egg yellow with a chunk of toast. As he finished chewing, he rubbed his mouth and whiskers with a napkin. 'Well, that was real good. I'd better get going, now. Want to come along?'

'No, you go ahead. I'll try to finish the machete work, and then we can have the rest of the day free.'

She gave him a key to the front door, and kissed him good-bye. When he was gone, she cleaned up the kitchen. Then she returned to her bedroom. Her chest tightened as she reached for the curtain cord. She hesitated, then pulled. The curtains skidded open, letting sunlight fill the room, and she quickly looked out.

Nobody there.

Of course not.

The back yard was deserted, the pool's surface pale blue and motionless, nothing on the diving board. Breathing more easily, she made the bed. She hung her robe on the closet door, cleaned herself up in the master bathroom, then got dressed in cut-off jeans and a baggy, sleeveless sweatshirt. She slipped into thongs, and made her way through the silent house.

The aroma of bacon lingered in the kitchen. She glanced out the window. Her Rabbit stood alone on the driveway, as if abandoned. Other cars were parked on the street.

No hearse.

She stepped to the side door, entered her garage, and turned on the overhead light. Shutting the door, she wished for a way to lock it from this side.

If he broke into the house . . .

She realised that none of her doors locked from both sides. You could lock someone out of the house, but not inside. You might secure yourself within a bathroom or bedroom, but there was no way to seal the doors from the other side.

Dani saw the workings of a benevolent, misguided hand.

No, no, no, thou shalt not lock thy child in his bedroom.

And thou shalt not take refuge in thy garage.

Probably a goddamn law against it. Probably in the building code.

Screw it, she thought. I'm gonna put a bolt on that sucker.

She would have to buy one, first.

Today.

But not just now. The first priority was business. Dani stepped over to her workbench and picked up the foam latex face of Bill Washington. He was to be the second victim, nonchalantly drinking a beer when the maniac leaped from the porch roof and whacked him across the forehead with a machete.

Jack would be wielding the machete, swinging it with enough force to penetrate the forehead of the appliance. The catcher's mask beneath would cushion the blow for Bill.

Dani pulled up a stool. The glass eyes seemed to watch her, as if mildly curious, as she fitted the face over the metal cage of the catcher's mask. She determined where it needed more padding. With an Exacto knife, she cut pieces from a mat of foam rubber. She glued them inside the chin, the cheeks, behind the eyes. She pushed blood-bags behind the forehead, then glued a patch of rubber over them. When the face fit snug against the tubing of the mask, she glued it in place.

With calipers, she measured the width of the forehead at the angle they'd decided the machete would strike. She marked off the distance on a sheet of poster board, and snipped out a crescent. She tried the cut-away cardboard on the face. The cut was too shallow. She took off another quarter inch, and again pressed it to Bill's brow.

Fine.

Stretching over the workbench, she picked up the two machetes. They looked identical, vicious weapons with worn wooden handles. But one weighed only a few ounces while the other dragged her arm down. Except for the handle, taken from a real machete, the lighter of the pair was constructed of balsa wood. Jack had done a good job. The paint gleamed like steel, shiny in the same places as the other, mottled with rust near the hilt, a few nicks on the edge.

A work of art.

Dani hated to tamper with it.

But if she didn't, Jack would have to take time when he returned. He'd be glad to have it done.

So she pressed the cardboard cut-out against the blade, and traced its crescent with a pencil. Carefully, she whittled down to the line. The machete looked as if a large bite had been taken out of it.

She pressed it, at an angle, against the mask's forehead.

It fit well.

After the real blow, the mask would be removed, the balsa machete glued to Bill's own forehead, and makeup applied. Cameras rolling again, he'd quiver and shake and slump.

End of effect.

With the proper camera angles, lighting and editing, it should look like poor Bill actually caught a blade in the face.

Smiling, Dani brushed the balsa curls off her sweatshirt.

She was out by the pool, stretched on a chaise longue with the sun pressing warm on her back, when the sliding door from the bedroom rumbled open. Her stomach jumped. She raised her head and saw Jack come out.

'Sorry it took so long.'

'That's all right.'

He walked forward, his swimming trunks hanging low on his hips, a towel under one arm. 'Had a couple of errands to run.'

'I just got out here. Finished up with Bill and the machete.'

'How do they look?'

'Just great.'

'So we're all set for tomorrow?'

'All set. The rest of the day is for play.'

With a grin, he flopped his towel onto the patio chair beside Dani. 'How's the water?'

'Let's find out.'

# EIGHT

BLESS MY soul! How are you, honey?'

'Just fine,' Linda said, nodding pleasantly to the buxom, grinning woman behind the counter.

'Mighty good to see you up and around.'

'Thank you, Elsie.' She turned to the paperback rack, scanning the covers.

'You look real good. How's the leg?'

'Good as new, almost.'

'We were all just worried to death about you. 'Specially when we heard you was in one of them comas. I read me a book about a fella in a coma. He was dead to the world, oh, 'bout ten years.' Elsie leaned over the counter, her eyes widening. 'When he come to, he could see in the future. Gave him no end of trouble.'

'I wouldn't mind that,' Linda said.

'More a curse than a gift, you ask me.'

'Well, it didn't happen to me, so I guess I'll never know.' She slipped a book from the rack and carried it to the counter.

Elsie picked it up. 'Oh dear, that's a scary one. Did you read the other?'

'I sure did.'

'Them Bradleys, they had no end of trouble.' Elsie rang it up. 'You hear the news about our own haunted house?'

'The Freeman place?'

'Got burnt to the ground last night. Elwood Jones was in for his *Post*, told me all 'bout it. He's on the volunteers, you know.'

Linda nodded. She put a hand on the counter to steady herself.

'Yessir, burnt to the ground. That's three seventy-eight, with tax.'

56

Linda opened her purse. Her hands trembled as she took out her billfold.

In a hushed voice, Elsie said, 'There was two bodies in it, burnt to a crisp.'

'My God,' Linda muttered.

'They figure one's Ben Leland's boy, Charles. Couldn't tell by looking, but he's turned up missing and they say he takes his girlfriends in there for some foolishness – though, Lord knows, you wouldn't catch *me* in there after dark. Nor in broad daylight, neither.' She took the bills from Linda and counted out the change. 'Elwood, he says they don't know who the gal is yet. Larson, down by the morgue, he's gonna have to go by her teeth.' Elsie slipped the book and receipt into a bag. 'Real bad business, but that's what comes of fooling where you don't belong. Least the Freeman place is gone, now. That's a blessing.'

'Yes it is,' Linda said.

'You have a good day, now, and don't make yourself a stranger.'

'Thanks, Elsie,' She took the bag. With a wave, she turned away and headed for the door.

Outside, the heat wrapped her like a blanket. She stayed close to the store fronts, welcoming the shade of their awnings as she walked up the block.

Charles Leland. He'd been two years ahead of her in school, and she knew him only slightly. He wasn't the one who'd come after her with the ax, though. Not unless he'd been wearing weird makeup or a mask. That was too bad. She would've liked to burn up that man along with the house.

She realised she ought to feel guilty. Maybe she would, if she'd known him. But Elsie was right: he had no business being there. It was his own damn fault. Nobody to blame but himself.

Must've used a key from his father. That's why the back door wasn't locked.

Linda hoped the girl wasn't anyone she knew.

At the corner, she slipped the paperback out of its bag. She crumpled the bag and receipt, and tossed them into a trash bin marked KEEP CLAYMORE BEAUTIFUL.

Walking along, she creased the book's cover. She opened it to the middle and flexed the halves backwards. Turning to other

57

sections, she bent the book again and again. By the time she reached the corner, the spine was streaked with white veins as if the book had been read more than once.

For good measure, she turned down a point of the cover. Then she slipped the book into her purse.

She turned at Craven Street. Passing Hal's house, she kept her eyes on the sidewalk.

If he'd shown up at the library that night . . .

But she couldn't blame him. He had no way to know she was waiting for him, wanting him.

A door banged shut and she halted, her heart racing. He'd seen her pass by! *I've wanted you so long, Linda*. His embrace would wash her clean and take away all the pain and she would be as she was before the Freeman house.

'Hi Linda.'

She whirled around. Hal's smile pierced her. He was tanned and handsome in his T-shirt and faded cut-offs, a lock of golden hair falling across his forehead. 'Hi Hal,' she said.

'How's the leg?'

'Fine, thank you.'

With a wink, he turned away. He hurried around the front of his Z car, and climbed in.

Linda's smile fell off.

The car lunged away from the curb. At the end of the block, it turned left and vanished.

Linda took a deep, shaky breath. She gritted her teeth to stop the trembling of her chin. The sidewalk blurred. She wiped the tears out of her eyes, but new ones came.

'Who needs him,' she muttered. She'd hardly given him a thought since the accident. If she hadn't been stupid enough to walk by his house . . .

He could've stopped all this.

He doesn't know. He'll never know.

Linda wiped her eyes dry and put on her sunglasses.

Two blocks later, she reached Tony's house. She turned up its walkway. A cat hopped onto the porch glider, setting it into creaky motion. From the back yard came the chatter of a lawn mower.

She walked in the shade between the side of the house and its garage. The air smelled of cut grass. She plucked her clinging blouse away from her back, but it stuck again. She wiped a hand on her skirt, then took the paperback from her purse.

From the rear corner, she saw a young man striding behind a mower. He appeared to be about twenty. He was taller than Tony, lean but not emaciated. His bare torso was glossy with sweat. His jeans hung below the band of his white underwear, and looked as if they might drop off.

Turning the mower for another sweep, he briefly faced Linda. His frown changed to a look of vague curiosity. He finished the turn and started away, his head swiveling to keep an eye on her.

Linda waved the book. 'Hey!'

He shut off the lawn mower, but didn't let go of it. He squinted at Linda over his shoulder.

'I'm looking for Tony,' she called.

'He ain't here.' Turning away, he bent down and grabbed the starter cord.

'Wait,' Linda said.

With a shrug, he straightened up. He watched Linda approach as if she were an odd species he couldn't quite identify. Before she got too close, he sidestepped to put the lawn mower between them.

'You're Tony's brother, aren't you?'

He nodded. His gaze lowered to the front of her blouse.

'I'm Beth Emory.'

He continued to stare.

'Tony let me borrow this book of his,' she said. 'I'd like to see that he gets it back.'

'He ain't here.'

'I know. I heard he left town right after graduation.'

'Hasn't come back.'

'Do you know where he went?'

The man's tongue darted out, lapped speckles of sweat from over his lip. 'Huh-uh.'

'If I had his address, I'd mail it to him.'

'Don't know where he went to.'

'Does your mother know?'

'Huh-uh.'

'Is she home now?'

His head shook slowly from side to side, his gaze remaining on Linda's breasts. 'Mom, she's been dead ten years this August.'

'Oh. I'm sorry. I didn't know.'

'You wanta leave that book, it's all right. Maybe he'll come back. You don't never know, with Tony.'

'I have to know where he is,' Linda said. She felt a sickening tightness in her chest, but didn't let it stop her. With trembling fingers, she flicked open the top button of her blouse. 'You can tell me.'

His shallow chest rose and fell. A hand went up to wipe his mouth.

Linda opened the next button. 'You know where he is, don't you?'

'Go 'way,' he whispered.

'Tell me.'

'I don't . . . ' He shook his head sharply.

Linda opened the button at her belly, and spread the blouse wide. She squeezed the stiff cups of her bra. 'Tell me. Tell me and you can see.'

'He . . . he's in California.'

'Where?'

'Hollywood.'

'What's his address?'

'Don't know.'

She unhooked the front of the bra and lifted it away. 'Tell me. Tell me, and you can feel.'

He stared. He licked his lips. 'I don't knooow.'

'Yes you do.' She caressed her breasts, squeezed them.

'I . . . oh, *oh*! Go away!' Doubling over, he turned away and fell to his knees. He grabbed his groin. His forehead pounded the grass.

Linda stared, astonished and disgusted.

Clutching her blouse shut, she ran.

# NINE

DANI ADDED a splash of milk, and set the pot back onto the barbeque grill. She stirred the creamy potatoes with a wooden spoon. After a few strokes, the heat became too much. She backed away, rubbing the hot skin of her belly.

'That hungry?' Jack asked.

'That burnt.'

He swung himself off the lounger, stepped up beside her, and sipped his vodka and tonic as he peered into the pot. 'Looking good,' he said.

'They're a real calorie bomb, but what the hell? We deserve it, right?' A few bubbles plopped to the surface. Dani reached out and stirred, the heat curling against the underside of her arm. 'I think we're about ready for the steaks.'

'I'm more than ready.'

'You want to keep an eye on this? Just stir it a bit.'

With a nod, he took the spoon in his free hand.

'Refill while I'm in?'

'Sure, thanks.' He tilted his glass back. The cubes broke loose from the bottom and dropped against his face, splashing him. He gasped with surprise. 'It fights back,' he said. He backhanded a drip off the tip of his nose, rubbed his wet mustache and beard.

'What poise,' Dani said.

'My specialty.'

She took his glass, picked hers up from the tray, and slid open the screen door to the living room. The carpet felt good after the rough concrete. The house was cool, almost chilly against her sun-heated skin.

She slid the glasses to the other side of the bar counter and wiped her wet hands across her belly, leaving dark trails on her skin. Rarely had she felt so fine: light and compact, glowing with the sun and two vodkas and her new closeness with Jack.

She stretched, sighing at the luxury of her aching muscles. They were tight and vibrant from so much swimming and from the long love-making earlier in the afternoon. The feel of Jack was still inside her.

Makes a lasting impression, she thought, and smiled.

Then she stepped around the counter to fill the drinks. She was carrying ice cubes when the telephone rang. She dumped the cubes into the glasses, flinched as she wiped her cold hands on her sides, and hurried to the end of the bar. She grabbed the phone.

'Hello?'

'Hello, Danielle.' The voice sounded young and ugly and almost familiar.

It made her stomach tighten. 'Yes?'

'Do you know who *this* is?'

'Not offhand,' she said, wondering if he were an acquaintance trying to be funny. 'Want to give me a clue?'

'Last night,' he whispered. In the pause, she heard him breathing. 'The restaurant. The death buggy.'

A cramp seized her stomach, and her legs went weak. She hunched over the counter, elbows bracing her. 'Who . . . who are you?'

'The Chill Master.'

'Huh?'

'I frighten people.' He spoke slowly, as if savoring the menace in his voice. 'I give them goosebumps. I make them wet their pants. I make them scream in terror.'

'You make them hang up,' Dani said, and hung up. She sagged off the bar top and crouched down, hugging her belly. The peal of the telephone jolted her. It rang again and again. She covered her ears. 'Stop,' she whispered.

And then she saw herself as if from a distance, huddled down and cowering.

Just what the Chill Master ordered.

She suddenly felt abused. Anger shoved her fear aside. She stood up straight and picked up the phone. 'Hello,' she snapped.

'Hello, Danielle.'

'What do you want?'

'Have I frightened you?'

'Yes. Happy?'

'Oh yes.'

'Good. How about getting out of my life?'

'But that's the whole point, Danielle. I want *into* your life. How did you like my surprise?'

'I don't like anything about you.'

'That's not nice.'

'I don't like being attacked at dinner, and I don't like being followed, and I don't like being spied on . . .'

'You're beautiful naked.'

'And you're gonna be in big trouble if you don't stop messing with me.'

'You shouldn't be mad, Danielle. You should be flattered that I chose you.'

'I'm not.'

'I could've chosen from so many others, you know. But I chose you.'

'What are you talking about?'

'I'm going to be your apprentice.'

It all suddenly fell into place. 'Last night . . . everything . . . was your idea of an audition?'

'Yes, yes, *yes*! My way of introduction to the queen of horror makeup effects. Wasn't I brilliant?'

'Terrific,' she muttered.

'When do I start?'

'Start what?'

'Working with you. We'll be wonderful together. We'll set the world aflame!'

'I already have an assistant.'

'Fire him.'

'Not hardly.'

'But you admitted I scared you,' he said, his voice rising.

'That's not the point.'

'It *is* the point! I'm a genius! Nobody can frighten people like I can. I'm the Chill Master. You'll be famous for discovering me.'

'Sorry.'

'You don't think I'm *good enough*?'

'I don't need an assistant,' she said.

'You didn't like my head?'

'It was fine.'

'It was great!'

'Look, I have to go. I'm sorry I can't help you.'

'I want it back.'

'Okay. Give me your address and I'll mail it.'

'I'll come for it. Tonight.'

'No!'

'Scared?' he asked. Then he hung up.

Dani finished mixing the drinks, and carried them outside. Th[e] sight of Jack stirring the potatoes was comforting. He turned [to] accept his drink, and frowned. 'What's wrong?'

'The telephone.'

'I heard it ring.'

She took a swallow of her vodka and tonic. 'It was our frien[d] from last night. He's apparently a horror freak who wants [to] apprentice under me.'

'Oh boy,' Jack muttered.

'Didn't know I was that famous. He called me "the queen [of] horror makeup effects." '

'He probably read the *Fangoria* article.'

'You're right. I hadn't . . . that'd explain how he recognise[d] me, too.'

Jack shook his head, scowling into his drink. 'So, he followe[d] us here so he could deliver a sample of his work . . . '

'And to prove how scary he is.'

'The bastard sounds like a mental case.'

'He really flew off the handle when I told him to get lost.'

'Did he say who he is?'

'Sure. He's the Chill Master. I tried to get his name an[d] address, but . . . Ready for this? He's coming over tonight f[or] his head.'

'Good.'

'Jack . . . '

'He'll have to trade in his hearse for a wheelchair.'

64

'Let's just leave the head out for him, and go to a movie or something.'

Jack shook his head.

'He's just a harmless nut.'

'He's a menace, Dani.'

'All he did . . . '

'Do you *realise* all he did?'

'He scared the hell out of me last night, and . . . '

'How did he get your telephone number?'

'I don't . . . '

'You're not in the book. It's unlisted, so he didn't get it from an operator.'

'Then how?' she asked, her voice a shaky whisper.

'It's on the phone labels.'

'Huh?'

'He read it off one of your phones. He's been inside the house.'

# TEN

'How ABOUT here?' Heather asked.

'Let's go one more,' Steve said. The movie theater wasn[
crowded, so he thought it would be bad manners to settle dow[
right in front of the couple already seated. They stepped to th[
next row. 'Is this all right?' he asked.

'Fine.'

'Do you want the aisle?'

'It doesn't matter.'

Steve preferred the aisle seat so he could stretch out his leg[
If he took it, though, a stranger might sit down on the other sid[
of Heather. He wouldn't like that. Heather wouldn't, eithe[
Since both the seats in front of them were vacant, the view woul[
be fine from either position.

He stepped into the row, giving the aisle seat to Heather. Sh[
smoothed her skirt against the backs of her legs and sat dow[
The skirt left her knees bare. She was wearing no nylons.

'Which show's first?' she asked.

'*Eyes of the Maniac,* I think.'

She drew up her shoulders and made herself shiver.

'Hope it's not goo gory for you.'

'The gorier, the better,' she said.

He gave Heather one of the Pepsis and a straw.

'Did you see the one where the girl got scalped?' she asked.

'Yeah.'

'A real gross-out.' She tore off an end of the straw's wrappe[
slid the thin paper sheath down a bit, and twisted the other en[
'I used to shoot these, did you?'

'Yeah.'

'It's so juvenile, though.'

66

Steve shrugged.

With a laugh, she blew the wrapper at him. It streaked past his cheek and landed on the next seat.

He held out his own straw. 'Try again?'

'Why not? You're only sixteen once, as Dad always says.' She aimed at Steve and puffed. He shut his eyes. The wrapper tapped his eyelid and fell. 'Oh *no*. You all right?'

'Sure.'

She lowered her head and gazed at him from under her curtain of brown bangs, sheepish but grinning. 'Sor-ry.'

'I can take it.'

She gave his straw back. He jabbed it through the X on the plastic top of his Pepsi. The tip had a pink smear from Heather's lipstick. He put his mouth on it.

Where her mouth had been.

It gave him a warm feeling. Almost like a kiss. He'd never kissed Heather, but tonight, when he took her home, he would try.

He sucked in a sip of Pepsi. When he slid the straw from his mouth, he could taste her lipstick.

Would she let him kiss her? It was their first date, and . . . yeah, she would. She must like him all right or she wouldn't be here.

She reached for a handful of popcorn, making the tub push down slightly on his lap. The feel of it made him want to squirm.

He took some popcorn. As he munched it, he watched her. She was bent over slightly, head down, eating out of her cupped hand.

Her blouse gaped like a slanted mouth in the space between two buttons. It showed a shadowy slope of skin, a lacey white corner of bra. Steve stared, suddenly dry-mouthed, his heart kicking, a hot surge swelling his penis.

Then the lights dimmed.

He looked away, relieved but disappointed, certain that nothing on the movie screen could match what he'd spied through the peephole of Heather's blouse.

She reached into the popcorn tub. The slight pressure was almost too much. Steve crossed his legs to ease the tightness.

Pepsi washed the dryness from his mouth. He licked his lips, but the flavor of her lipstick was gone.

A preview for *Death Grin* came on.

'Oooh,' Heather whispered. 'That looks neat.'

'Yeah.' Maybe he would bring her back when it played here.

A man dropped into the seat in front of Heather. The jerk. With all these empty seats . . .

'Can you see all right?' Steve asked.

'It's okay.'

'Want to trade places?'

'Well . . . Let's just move over one.'

They did.

The jerk scooted down and propped his knees against the back of the chair in front of him. A dark stocking cap covered his head. Steve saw no fringe of hair, and wondered if the guy was bald; he looked too young to be bald. Maybe shaves his head. Only a real jerk would shave his head.

Steve looked back at the screen as the film started.

A woman was taking a shower, humming as she soaped herself. Her back and rump were slick with streaming water. She turned round. Steve gazed at her small, glossy breasts, her nipples, the wedge of dark hair at her groin. He felt a warm stir, but it didn't compare with the jolt of desire at his stolen glimpse of Heather.

The woman turned away. She shut off the faucets. She slid open the shower curtain. Heather jumped as a shriek of music blasted through the theater and hands in leather gloves thrust a fireplace poker into the woman's belly. The point broke her skin, went in deep, hook and all. As the music screamed, she was rammed backwards against the shower wall. The gloved hands twisted the poker. Blood spilled from her mouth. Then the poker was pulled out slowly, the point of its hook stretching her flesh below the original wound, popping through, ripping open a flap of skin and dragging out slippery coils of guts.

Heather turned her head. Her eyes were squeezed shut. She opened one and looked at Steve. 'Is it over yet?'

'Just about.'

'Geez!'

'Okay, it's over.'

She turned her head, slumped low in her seat and sighed.

The man in the next row looked around, grinning. His face was pale and bony, his eyes hardly visible in the shadows of their sockets. 'Great effects, huh?'

'Yeah,' Steve muttered.

Heather nodded. She sat up straight and leaned away from the stranger.

'Know who did it? Danielle Larson.'

'A woman?' Steve asked.

'The queen of horror makeup. I work with her, you know.'

'You do?'

'Wonderful lady. Beautiful, too.'

'That's very interesting.'

'You think this is good, you should see our next film. It'll scare the shit out of you.'

Steve nodded. He took a deep breath when the young man turned away. The stiffness went out of Heather. She looked up at Steve, rolled her eyes, then settled her head against his shoulder. She kept it there while she sipped her Pepsi, ate popcorn, watched the movie. Sometimes, her hair tickled Steve's cheek.

On the screen, five young women were gathered for the funeral of their friend.

'They're all gonna get it,' Heather said.

'All but one.' The talking eased his nerves.

'Yeah. I bet it's the blonde with the freckles.'

'Yeah,' he said, wiping his oily hand on a napkin. His stomach fluttered. 'Okay if . . . ?' he mumbled, and curled his arm around her shoulders. Her head returned as if nothing had happened. He squeezed her shoulder gently. Then, for a long time, he didn't move his hand. He'd made a big move, and needed time to get used to it.

'Uh-oh,' Heather said.

One of the five, a slim brunette, had let her boyfriend stop at a lover's lane.

'They're gonna get it now,' Heather said.

Steve gave her shoulder another squeeze as if to comfort her.

The pair in the front seat were hugging, moaning as they kissed with open mouths. Then the man unbuttoned her blouse. She was wearing no bra.

Steve's thumb stroked the bra-strap through Heather's blouse.

Her breasts were blue-gray in the darkness of the car, her nipples almost black. The man quickly covered them with his hands.

They writhed against each other, gasping.

'Any second,' Heather said.

She flinched as something tapped the windshield.

Steve stroked her upper arm.

The woman raised her eyes to the windshield and screamed.

Heather jumped. She clutched Steve's leg.

A gloved fist smashed through the windshield, caught the woman by her hair, jerked her from the arms of her stunned lover and pulled her head through the jagged hole. The glass slashed bloody streaks down her face. The maniac, dressed in black and wearing a ski mask, leaped up and down on the car's hood like a frenzied gorilla, hanging onto her hair, tugging the head from side to side until finally the windshield cut it free. He hugged the severed head to his chest and ran off into the forest while the man inside the car stared at the pumping neck stump of his girlfriend and screamed.

Steve loosened his grip on Heather's shoulder. She let go of his leg, but her hand stayed there, a warm pressure.

The man in the next row looked back at them. 'Tore it right off, huh?'

'Yeah,' Steve said.

Heather reached for more popcorn.

'Yeah, right off. Can I have some of that?'

'Popcorn?' Steve asked.

'Let me have some. You don't need all that.' He reached over the back of the seat. His hand hovered over Heather's knees. She stiffened. Steve thrust the tub under it, and he grabbed a fistful. He shoved the popcorn into his mouth and dug into the tub again.

'Come on,' Steve said. 'We're trying to watch the movie.'

The young man made a mocking smile as he chewed. He reached in, took a third handful, then turned away.

Heather let out a shaky breath. She leaned closer to Steve and whispered, 'Let's move.'

He nodded. He felt shaky himself: angry and embarrassed and somehow frightened, just as he felt when accosted on the street by bums wanting handouts.

Heather took the popcorn tub. 'Want any more?' she asked.

'No way. Not after he's touched it.'

She set it on the uptilted seat beside her.

They stood up. Though their cushions squeaked, the man didn't turn. They stepped into the aisle and walked five rows back. 'This okay?' Steve whispered.

'Fine.'

They moved in, excusing themselves as they squeezed past a seated couple, and sat down near the center of the row. In front of them, two teenaged girls were slumped low, their heads well out of the way.

Heather sighed.

'Better?' Steve asked.

'A lot.'

'Me too.'

'What a creep,' she said. She finished her Pepsi and set it on the floor. Then she took hold of Steve's hand.

'Want me to buy some more popcorn?'

'No thanks. I had plenty.'

On the screen, one of the women was running through dark woods, whimpering, glancing over her shoulder. She was missing a sleeve. She stumbled and fell, scurried to her feet and kept running. Finally, she ducked behind a tree. She peered into the darkness, apparently looking for her pursuer.

The woods were silent. Nothing moved. The woman looked relieved. She stepped backwards away from the trunk. A vague blur appeared behind her shoulder – the masked face of the maniac.

Heather's hand tightened.

The woman continued backwards, gazing ahead, moving closer and closer to the waiting man.

People in the audience yelled warnings. Some squealed.

The woman kept stepping backwards. Behind her, an ax raised high.

Heather screamed and leaped from her seat, hands flying to the back of her neck, trying to pry loose the clutching fingers. The man, still hanging on, laughed like a lunatic. His stocking cap was gone, his hairless head gleaming like a skull.

Steve swung at his jaw. He connected, snapping the man's head sideways. A set of white fangs burst from the open mouth. He swung again. This time, he missed. The man grabbed his arm and bit it.

An usher hurried up the row, yelling.

The man sprang away. He hurtled over the seat backs, and raced up the next row. Yelling people rushed to get out of his way. He got to the aisle, turned on the charging usher, and bellowed a scream.

The usher stopped fast.

With a wild laugh, he bounded up the aisle and smashed through the door.

Heather threw herself into Steve's arms, sobbing. 'Take me home. Please I want to go *home*!'

# ELEVEN

ALONE IN her living room with the curtains shut, Dani tried to read. Though her eyes moved over the words, her mind strayed. Again and again, she reached the bottom of a page only to realise she knew nothing of what had happened on it. Finally, she shut the book.

She opened the front door. From where she stood, the aspen near the corner of the lawn was a vague, black shadow. She stepped outside. She toed the grocery bag, denting in its side. It hadn't been disturbed. She left it on the lighted stoop and walked toward the aspen.

'Jack?' she asked softly.

There was no answer.

More than an hour ago, just after dark, he'd crouched behind the tree. 'A great place for an ambush,' he'd said, and smacked his open hand with a sawed off length of broomstick.

Dani's protests had been feeble. She wanted the boy punished, dissuaded from bothering her further, but she didn't like the idea of using violence against him. Jack had promised to hurt him only enough 'to get the message across.'

He was no longer behind the tree.

Dani looked down the hedge separating her lawn from the street. No sign of him. She peered along the dark shrubbery to the corner of her house where it met the redwood fence.

'Jack?'

No answer.

A cool trickle ran down her side. She rubbed it away with her sweatshirt and walked across the lawn toward the driveway. Jack's Mustang was still parked there beside her own car.

As she approached it, a pale blur appeared at the driver's

window. She halted, staring at it, her heart pounding hard.

'Jack? Is that you?'

The window rolled down. 'What's up?'

At the sound of Jack's voice, she sighed. 'I thought you were by the tree.'

'This is better.'

'Why don't you come in now?'

'What for?'

'I don't think this is such a great idea.'

'Dani, we agreed . . . '

'I know, but I changed my mind.' She pulled open the car door. The ceiling light came on, and Jack squinted in its brightness. 'Come on, let's go in.'

He climbed from the car and pushed the broomstick into his back pocket. 'Why do you want to give it up?'

'I've thought about it a lot. It's a bad idea, Jack. Let's just go inside. He can take his head back, and maybe that'll be the end of it.'

'And maybe not. He needs a lesson.'

Dani shoved the car door shut. 'Look, if you beat him up, we could get into all kinds of legal hassles. He might sue . . . '

'For Godsake, he's the one who . . . '

'It happens. It's not worth it to me.' She took Jack's arm and walked him toward the house. 'Besides, that's just a minor thing. What really worries me is escalation. Suppose you *do* beat him up? It'd probably just make him mad. It'd make *me* mad. I'd want revenge. Wouldn't you?'

'I guess so.'

'I'm afraid he might comeback again to even the score. Then *we'd* want to get back at *him,* and God only knows where it might end.'

'That's a risk involved, yes.'

'Well, let's just avoid it. So far, he hasn't done anything violent. As far as we know, he's harmless.'

'He broke into your house.'

'Maybe. But he didn't attack me. Hell, he doesn't want to hurt me, he wants a job. That could all change if we bash him around. We might *make* him dangerous.'

Jack shrugged. 'All right. We'll try it your way.'

'Thanks.' She squeezed his arm. They stepped around the grocery bag, and Jack pushed the front door open. Dani entered first, glimpsed the man pressed to the wall inside and jumped away with a gasp.

A low, mad laugh hissed through the mouth-hole of the ghoul mask. It stopped with a grunt as Jack's forearm rammed across the mask. His left fist jabbed hard into the boy's belly.

'That's enough,' Dani gasped. 'That's . . .'

Jack punched him once more, then stepped back. The boy slumped to a squat, clutching his belly and gasping.

Jack yanked the mask off.

Dani stared at the agonised face, the bone-white skin and tiny eyes, the lips peeled back over yellow teeth as he struggled for air. The head lowered. An eye, crudely drawn with marking pens, seemed to gaze at her from the center of his hairless crown.

'I'll watch him,' Jack said. 'You want to call the cops?'

Dani shook her head. 'What's your name?' she asked.

He looked up, glanced from Dani to Jack, to Dani again.

'If you co-operate,' she said, 'Maybe we won't call the police. Now, what's your name?'

'Anthony.'

'Anthony what?'

'Johnson.'

'Let's see your driver's license.'

He started to get up, but Jack shoved him down by the shoulder. Reaching into a rear pocket of his black pants, he took out a wallet. He flipped it open and held it out.

Dani took it. 'You're from New York.'

He nodded.

'How long have you been out here?'

'Five weeks.'

'He's just eighteen,' she told Jack.

'Good. Old enough to be tried as an adult.'

'Let's go in the living room and sit down.'

'Dani . . .'

'We might as well be comfortable. It may take a while.'

'What?' Jack asked.

75

'We're going to defuse the situation.'

Anthony stared at Dani as if she were an intriguing animal. He got to his feet, and she gave his billfold back.

She led the way into the living room. Anthony followed, with Jack close behind him. 'You've been in here before,' she said.

'I didn't take anything.'

She nodded towards an easy chair. Anthony sat down.

'When and how did you get in?'

'This morning. You were in the pool, and left the back door open.' He seemed quite pleased with himself.

'The bedroom door?'

He nodded.

He must've passed within yards of her. While she swam, thinking she was alone, thinking she was safe even as he spied on her and sneaked into her house.

'Why did you do it?' Jack asked.

'Why not?'

'Wipe that smirk off your face.'

He wiped it off with his hand.

'Why?' Dani asked.

'I've got my reasons.'

Jack, tight with anger, looked at Dani as if asking permission to stomp the young man.

'Why don't you get us some drinks?' she asked. 'Anthony, would you like a beer?'

His head bobbed.

Jack's head tipped sideways and he regarded Dani with amazement.

'It's all right,' she said. 'I'm not crazy.'

'It's *your* party.' He made a smile at Anthony. 'Would you prefer Coors, Bud, or Dos Equis?'

'Coors.'

He glanced at Dani, rolled his eyes upward, and walked toward the bar.

Dani sat on the sofa. Elbows propped on her knees, she stared at Anthony. 'Did you do it to get my phone number?'

'Nooo.'

'You want to work with me, right? You want to learn the

ropes, get started on a makeup career?'

He nodded.

'Then we have to trust each other.'

'You said you didn't want me.'

'Maybe I'll change my mind. You obviously have a certain talent for frightening people.'

'Oh I do.'

'Tell me about it.'

He leaned forward, bracing his elbows on his knees, his chin on his fists. The same position as Dani. She noticed the similarity, wondered if it was intended to mock her. But she didn't move.

'I've always liked scary films.'

'Why?'

'They're fun. People jump and scream.'

'In the audience?'

'On the screen, too. It's a blast.'

'These films, do they scare you?'

His tiny eyes widened. 'The good ones do.'

'How do they make you feel?'

'Tight and shaky. I get goosebumps all over and want to scream.' He lowered his hands, rubbed them, glanced toward the bar. 'I get that way when *I* scare people, too.'

'You frighten yourself?'

'It's fantastic.'

'Do you do that much, go around trying to throw a fright into people – and into yourself?'

'All the time.'

Jack returned. He handed a can of Coors to Anthony, then sat down beside Dani and gave her a bottle of Dos Equis. 'What'd I miss?' he asked, and smiled wildly as if eager to join the madness.

'Anthony was just explaining how he likes to frighten people.'

'That sounds like fun. It must be especially nice for his victims.'

'I never hurt anyone,' he whispered as if sharing a wonderful secret.

'You just like to make them squirm?'

'I like to make them *scream*.'

'Sort of a hobby.'

77

'Hobby?' He sniggered. He took a sip of beer, settled back and crossed his legs. 'I'm the Chill Master. Once I've become famous for my horror effects, I'll move into the production end. I'll make films that'll send audiences shrieking from the theaters.'

'Nice to meet a fellow with ambition,' Jack said.

Dani frowned at him, smiled at Anthony. 'Basically, then, you want someone to start you on the way.'

'Exactly,' he said. He took a sip of beer. 'Who better than the queen of horror makeup effects?'

'You read the *Fangoria* article?' Jack asked.

'Oh yes. And I've seen all Danielle's films. She's better than Savini.'

'Thank you,' Dani said.

'How did you find her?'

Looking pleased with himself, Anthony took out his billfold. He removed a thick mat of paper from the bill compartment, and snapped off its rubber band. He unfolded the pack. 'My collection,' he said. He peeled off a color photo apparently snipped from a magazine, and held it up. At this distance, the bearded face resembled Jack.

'Rob Bottin,' Anthony said. He showed them another. 'Dick Smith. And here's Rick Baker. Tom Savini. Danielle Larson.'

Dani stared at the photo. It came from the *Fangoria* article.

Smiling, Anthony started to put his collection back together. 'I know all your faces. I've spent the last month keeping my eyes open, hanging around the studios and the "in" restaurants and bars. I knew I'd find one of you sooner or later.'

'You're very persistent,' Dani said.

'And innovative,' Jack added.

'I'm glad it was you I found. You're the best. And the most beautiful.'

*You're beautiful naked.*

'We'll make a great team,' Anthony said.

'I'm sure of it.'

Jack gaped at her.

Dani ignored him. 'We're busy tomorrow. Why don't you come over on Saturday? We'll show you a few things, get you started.'

'Honest?'

'Yep.'

'What time?'

'In the morning. How about nine?'

'Great!'

'There's only one condition.'

He sank back in his chair, looking suddenly dejected.

'No more bugging us. That means creeping around, following us, trespassing, spying on us. None of that. Otherwise, it's all off. Okay?'

'Sure!' He grinned, pounded the arm of the chair, and raised his beer can high. 'To Danielle Larson. You're the greatest!'

In his boyish enthusiasm, he seemed almost human.


Dani leaned against the door and shut her eyes, relieved to be rid of the strange boy. But he would be back. 'Do you think I'm nuts?'

'Definitely. Haven't you ever heard the age-old adage?'

'Which one?'

'Don't feed it, maybe it'll go away.' Jack stepped close to her, held her by the shoulders, kissed her forehead. 'That guy,' he whispered, 'is a lunatic.'

'I know.'

She moaned as Jack's hands slipped inside her sleeve holes and rubbed her shoulders.

'Do you feel sorry for him?'

'Hell no,' Dani said. 'He scares me.'

'Then why did you encourage him?'

'I want him to be with us, not against us. You be nice to him Saturday, okay?'

'I'll be charming.'

The hands squeezed warmth into Dani's tight, aching muscles.

'I've got one request,' Jack said.

'Uh-huh?'

'Don't ever let him in the house when I'm not here.'

'You can bet on it.'

# TWELVE

FROM HER car parked across the street, Linda saw Joel leave his house. He started up the sidewalk, striding fast and swinging his arms high. His lips were moving. He was either singing or talking to himself.

Linda started her car. She pulled forward, turned around at the end of the block, and drove up beside Joel. He jumped at the beep of her horn, but kept on walking.

'Hey Joel, want a ride?'

Turning, he ducked his head and raised his sunglasses. He squinted out from under the dark lenses. 'Linda?'

'Yeah. Where you going?'

'The pharmacy.'

'Hop in. I'll give you a lift.'

'Oh, that's all right.'

'Come on.' Leaning across the seat, she swung open the passenger door.

'Well . . . ' He shrugged, then loped over and climbed in. 'Thanks a lot,' he said. He slammed the door shut so hard the car shook. 'I don't want to put you out.'

'I was going that way, anyhow.'

'Well, thanks.'

She started the car forward. 'Besides, it's nice to have some company. I haven't seen many of the kids since the accident.'

'Yeah.' He nodded, staring straight ahead. 'That was too bad about your accident.'

'Those things happen.'

'You feeling all right, now?'

'Fine, thank you.'

'Good. That's good.' He rubbed his hands on his Bermuda

80

shorts. He rested an elbow on the window sill. 'This sure beats walking.'

'It's hot out there.'

'Yeah. Sure is.'

'It'll be real nice over at the river.'

'Yeah, probably.'

'I'm on my way over there.'

'Yeah?'

Linda gestured over her shoulder. Joel glanced around at the back seat.

'Gonna have a picnic?'

'Sure am. I've got fried chicken in there, and beer in the cooler.'

'Beer?'

'I've got plenty. How would you like to come along?'

'Geez, I don't know.'

'Come on. It'll be great.'

'I'd better not. I have to pick up this stuff for Mom.'

'Oh. Is she sick?'

'No, but . . .'

'If it's nothing that urgent, you could just get it later, couldn't you?'

'I guess, but I'd still better not.'

'Thanks,' Linda said.

He frowned at his knees.

'What, have I got leprosy?'

'No!'

She shook her head and tried to look sad. 'You probably think a girl like me has it made – a cheerleader, good grades, popular as hell. Well, I've got news, I'm a human being. I get hungry, just like everyone else. I sweat. I worry. I get horny. I get depressed. Believe it or not, sometimes I even get lonely.'

'You?'

'Yeah, me. The marvelous Linda Allison. Do you know who always asked me for dates? Jerks who thought they were God's gift to women. They were the only ones with guts enough to call. Do you think they cared about me as a person? They didn't give a damn about what's in my head or heart. They just cared about

81

what's under my clothes. If you want to know how lonely feels, you oughta find yourself parked in the woods with a guy who thinks you're a toy.'

'I'm sorry,' Joel said.

She stopped at the intersection. A right-hand turn would lead downtown, a left would take them toward the river. She stared at Joel. He looked confused and glum, but no longer nervous. 'Normal, nice guys – guys like you – never called.'

He shrugged.

'You thought I was too good for you?'

'Sort of.'

'You thought I'd laugh at you?'

'Maybe.'

Reaching out, Linda stroked his hand. 'Why would I laugh at you?'

He shook his head, and seemed to have a hard time swallowing.

'Come on, Joel. Let's go to the river. Please? I . . . I don't want to be alone.'

'Okay.'

She turned left.

The river, five miles north of town, curved through an area of dense forest. A portion of the woods had been cleared for the public, tables and barbeques set up, sand poured to make a small beach, a gravel parking lot laid. On summer days, it was usually aswarm with families, young couples, teenagers throwing Frisbees when they weren't swimming. At night, it became a place for romance.

Linda had been there often at night. Outside, on blankets. Inside cars. Usually as an eager participant. But she'd been with enough jerks to know how it felt being used – enough to convince Joel of her sorry plight.

As usual, the parking lot was crowded. She drove on by.

'Where's we going?' Joel asked, breaking the long silence.

'Up here a ways. I know a real nice place where there won't be a lot of people in our way.'

'Oh. Okay.' He patted his knees as if he needed to keep his hands busy.

'You don't mind, do you?'

82

'No. Wherever you want's fine with me.' He kept drumming his legs. He stared out the windshield, out the side window, down at his tapping hands. He looked everywhere except at Linda.

'No need to be nervous.'

'Me? I'm not nervous.'

'I don't bite, you know.'

'Just chicken?' he asked, and made a weak smile.

Linda forced herself to laugh.

Joel grinned and shrugged. 'Do you know why the chicken committed suicide?' he asked.

'No, why?'

'It didn't give a cluck.'

Linda laughed and shook her head.

'Wait. Wait, here's a good one. Do you know how to make a dead chicken float?'

'No.'

'First you get a dead chicken. Add a little ice cream, a little root beer . . . ' He started laughing.

'Oh, that's gross.'

'Yeah, isn't it? That's a good one. That's one of my favourites.'

Linda slowed down and swung onto the road's bumpy shoulder. 'Do you pluck it first?'

'No. The feathers are the best part.'

'Ish.'

They climbed from the car, Joel still laughing quietly. Linda opened the back door. She handed out the picnic basket and cooler. She grabbed her towel and faded red blanket, then led the way into the woods.

'Is the river very far?'

'Just two or three miles.'

He laughed some more. 'You know,' he said, 'you've got a good sense of humor.'

'Thank you. See, I told you I'm human.'

'Do you know what's green and red and goes thump, thump, thump?'

'No, what?'

'Kermit the Frog in a blender!'

He kept it up for the next fifteen minutes as they trudged

through undergrowth, climbed over deadfalls, ducked beneath low-hanging branches. Then they reached the river. Linda found a grassy clearing a few yards from the bank. She spread out the blanket.

She sat down on it, kicked off her sneakers, and stretched out her legs. 'Can you tell the difference?'

He shook his head.

'Take off your sunglasses.'

He lifted them, glanced at her legs, and shook his head again.

'This is the one,' she said. She patted her left thigh. 'See? It's not as tanned.'

'They both look fine.'

'You should've seen it when they took off the cast. All shriveled and white.'

He wrinkled his nose, lowered his sunglasses, and sat down to the far side of the basket and cooler.

'You ready for a beer?' Linda asked.

'Sure.'

She took two cans of Genesee from the cooler. She popped them open and handed one to Joel. 'Did you ever hear how it happened? My accident?'

'You got hit by a car?' His hand trembled slightly as he raised the can to his mouth.

'That's it. The thing is, I didn't look where I was going. Stupid, huh? Just ran right out into the street and *wham*.'

'Gosh.'.

She squinted as the top of her can flashed sunlight in her eyes. She took a long drink. 'Ready for some chicken?'

'Sure.'

She set aside her beer and opened the picnic basket. 'Sorry, I forgot the root beer and ice cream.'

He laughed a bit, sounding nervous again.

'What do you like: thighs, drumsticks, breasts?'

'I don't care.'

'I bet you're a breast man.'

He blushed, his pimply chin turning a deeper shade of red. 'Fine,' he told her.

Linda gave him a crispy breast and a napkin. She took out a

thigh for herself. 'It's really nice here, isn't it?' she asked. 'So quiet and private.'

'Yeah,' he said through a mouthful.

'Are you glad you decided to come?'

He smiled, and wiped his slick lips with a napkin. 'I sure am.'

They ate and drank in silence for a while. Linda opened two more cans of beer, passed another breast to Joel, nibbled on a drumstick. 'I don't hold it against you, you know.'

He stopped in mid-bite. 'Huh?'

'My accident. I don't hold any grudges.'

His sunglasses slipped down his nose. He poked them back with a greasy forefinger. 'I don't get it.'

'Sure you do. You were just having some fun. How could you know I'd be dumb enough to run in front of a car?'

He frowned. 'I still don't . . .'

'You, Arnold and Tony? The Freeman house? Jasper the friendly ghost?' She shook her head and laughed. 'I tell you, it scared the hell out of me. I thought sure ol' Jasper was going to cut my head off.'

'That was Tony,' he muttered.

'*Jasper* was Tony?'

'Yeah. He, uh, stayed behind. He had all that stuff upstairs . . . the makeup and phoney head. And the ax.'

'Figures,' she said, and wondered why she hadn't figured it out for herself. 'The whole thing was Tony's idea, I bet.'

'Yeah. We had a ladder around the back. He was planning to use that, but then you got knocked out . . .' Joel's chin started to tremble. 'Boy, I'm really sorry. I was a jerk to go along with him. Tony gets these crazy ideas.'

'It's all right. Don't worry about it. I didn't bring you out here to get into all that. I just thought . . . hell, you might be wondering about the whole thing, whether or not I recognised you. I just brought it up to let you know I'm not angry.' She took a drink of beer. 'Actually, it was a pretty neat idea. I wouldn't mind pulling it on someone, myself.'

'Really?'

'Someone like Tony.'

Joel laughed. Turning away, he took off his sunglasses and

wiped his eyes. 'Tony deserves it.'

'Of course, the Freeman house is no more.'

'Yeah, wasn't that something?'

'The paper said it was arson. I wonder if Tony did *that*.'

'No. He's gone. Didn't you know?'

'He is?'

'Yeah. He left after graduation. He went to Hollywood.'

'What's he doing there?'

'Wants to get into horror movies. He's always been big on those things, you know, but after what we did to you . . . I guess that made up his mind. He changed a lot, after that.'

'How do you know he's in Hollywood?'

'He keeps in touch with Arnold. They've been writing back and forth. He's trying to get Arnold to move out and join him.'

'Has he written to you?'

Joel shook his head. 'I sort of had it out with him. After what happened.'

'It bothered you that much?'

He nodded.

'That's really sweet, Joel.'

'I shouldn't have let him do it.'

'He just would've done it without you. More chicken?'

'No thanks.'

'How about another beer? We might as well finish them off.' She gave him a beer, popped hers open, took a drink, and rubbed the cool wet can against her face. 'Oh, that feels good.' She opened the top two buttons of her blouse. Joel looked away as she slipped the can inside. It felt icy on her breasts, made her nipples rigid. Unfastening another button, she slid the can across her belly. Joel, facing the river, gulped his beer. 'You should try it.'

He shrugged, and kept on drinking. Linda crawled over to him. 'No, it's . . .

'Lie back.'

'No, really . . . ' But he didn't resist as Linda pushed his shoulder. He eased backwards, stretching out his legs and holding his beer can at his side.

Linda knelt beside him. Leaning over, her blouse gaping, she plucked off his sunglasses. He glanced at her breasts and quickly looked up to her face. He flinched as she worked open a button of his shirt. 'Wh . . . ?'

'Won't hurt a bit,' she told him. Grinning, she continued to unfasten his shirt. His chest was hairless and pale. 'Ready?' He nodded. Linda pressed her beer can to his right nipple. He cringed, then laughed. 'See? Feels good, doesn't it?'

'Yeah.'

The can made a damp path down his skin. She slid it over his left nipple, then down his ribs. His belly sucked in at its cold touch. The front of his Bermudas bulged with the push of an erection.

'Roll over, I'll do your back.'

'This is weird,' he said.

'You like it, don't you?'

'Yeah,' he said, sitting up.

Linda helped him take his shirt off. Then he twisted around and lay down flat. He stiffened when she touched the can between his shoulder blades. She moved it slowly down his back, and up again, and then she upended it. Beer gurgled onto his shoulders.

'Hey!' he cried. He rolled away. Laughing, Linda pursued him on her knees, spilling beer onto his hair and face and chest. 'No! Don't!'

She stopped, and drank the final drops.

'Geez, you got it all over me!'

'Felt good, didn't it?'

'I'm a mess!' He wiped his chest, and glared at his hands. He looked as if he might cry.

'I'm sorry. I thought you'd like it.'

'I'm a mess.'

'You can do it to me,' she offered, and picked up Joel's can. She jiggled it. 'Half full. Come on.'

He shook his head.

'You want to, I can tell.'

'It's all right,' he said.

'Come on. Turn-about's fair play.'

'I don't want to get you messy.'

She set the can on the blanket near his knees. And then she took off her blouse.

Joel stared.

'Pour it on me,' she whispered.

Joel, looking dazed, picked up the can. He came forward on his knees.

'On my breasts,' she said.

Joel raised the can and tipped it. The cool beer splashed Linda's shoulder, washed over her breast, streamed around it, ran off the tip of her nipple. Joel gazed as if transfixed. He moved the can, and the beer spilled onto her other breast. It slid off, ran down her belly.

Moaning, Linda rubbed her breasts as if massaging the beer into them.

Joel poured until the can was empty.

Linda smiled and lowered her hands. 'Geez,' she said, 'you got it all over me. I'm a mess.'

His mouth twitched with something like a smile.

'I can't go home like this,' she said. 'I smell like a brewery.'

'Me too,' Joel said.

'We'd better wash it off,' she whispered.

He nodded, still gazing at her breasts. His eyes stayed with her as she stood up. They lowered, and his mouth dropped open when she unfastened her shorts.

'You gonna spend all afternoon catching flies,' Linda asked, 'or are you coming in?'

She kicked off her shorts and stood naked in front of him, feet apart, hands on hips, head tilted to one side. 'Well?'

He blinked. He licked his lips. He seemed to have a hard time breathing.

'Need help?'

He shook his head. 'Why . . . why don't you go on. I'll be there. In a minute.'

'All right, bashful.' She turned away and skipped down the grassy bank. Where the grass ended, the shore was rocky. She trod carefully over the stones, and waded into the water. It wrapped her legs, just cool enough to be refreshing. When it reached her thighs, she turned around.

Joel came down the slope, hunched over as if he were cold,

hands shielding the front of his striped boxer shorts. He walked gingerly over the stones.

'Hey,' Linda said, 'you don't want to get your shorts wet. How'll you explain it to your mother?'

He groaned. Turning away, he pulled them down. He pinned them to the ground with a rock, then backed toward the water. When it reached his knees, he dropped. He swung around and paddled for deeper water. Two yards from Linda, he stopped. He stayed low, covered to the shoulders, and stared up at her. He looked frightened but eager.

'Come here,' Linda said. 'Rinse the beer off me.'

'Geez.'

'Come on.'

He waddled toward her.

'Don't hide from me. Stand up straight.'

He rose from the water, holding his cupped hands over his groin.

'Splash me,' Linda whispered. 'Rub me. Get all the beer off.'

His hands dipped into the water, and he flung it up at her. He splashed her again and again, as if giving up his attempts to cover himself. His penis stood upright and rigid. With open hands, he stroked Linda's body. At first, he was business-like as if actually concerned about washing off the beer. But his hands began to linger on her breasts, sliding over them, fingering her stiff nipples, gently squeezing.

'Now you,' Linda said. She eased his hands away. They hung at his sides while she threw water onto his chest. She caressed him, her hands roaming lower, and finally her fingers curled around his erection. He gasped as they slid down it.

She let go.

'There,' she said. 'All clean.' With a laugh, she sprang away and dived. She clawed from rock to rock, pulling herself along the bottom. Then Joel grabbed her foot. She kicked free and surfaced. Joel popped from the water.

'I don't think we got all the beer off,' he said.

'Well well.' She stepped toward him through the neck-high water, and felt his hands on her breasts. She moved still closer. His erection prodded her belly. Squirming against it, she hooked her arms behind his back, kissed him. She brought her legs up wrapped them around him. 'Do you want me?' she whispered against his lips.

He only moaned.

Reaching down with one hand, she found his penis. It felt huge and warm. She held it, and lowered herself. It spread her, pushed into her, slid in deep. She hugged Joel tightly with her arms and legs, writhed, felt him penetrate even more.

His breath blew hard against her face. He held her more tightly and started to grunt, suddenly throbbing and pumping inside her, and jerked wildly, still coming, when Linda slammed the rock against the back of his head. He blinked, looking puzzled.

'That was your last wish,' Linda said, and struck again.

He tried to shove her away, but she clung with her legs and one arm, and pounded his head again.

He jerked at her hair.

The wig came off in his hand. He made a whimpering noise and she struck again, this time smashing the rock against his temple. His eyes rolled upward. He swayed. Linda shoved away from him, feeling an odd moment of loss when his penis left. She watched him go under. Tossing away the rock, she lunged for her floating wig. She shoved it onto her head, then went for Joel.

She found him a few inches under the surface, face down, arms and legs moving in a lazy way, hair stirring in the currents.

She curled her fingers through his hair, gripped it, and steered him lower. She rolled him onto his back. She guided him between her legs and clamped his head between her knees.

The river swirled around her. It pushed Joel, turned him slowly.

Finally, Linda opened her knees.

The body slipped away, feet first, and vanished in the murky water.

# THIRTEEN

'THE MACHETE has to go,' Roger said.

'What?'

'I know it's a drag, I know it's all set. We'll shoot around the splash scene and take it up on Monday.'

'What's wrong with the machete?' Dani asked.

'Not a thing. It's beautiful, beautiful.' He squeezed her shoulder as if to comfort her. 'But here's the thing, I caught *Friday the 13th Part II* on *ON* last night and there's a guy catches a machete in the face.'

'I know. I told you that a month ago.'

'No big deal, right? Instead of a machete, our boy catches an ax.' He turned away and yelled, 'Bruce! The ax!'

The prop master, standing across the set by the coffee machine, nodded and hurried off.

'Wait till you see it,' Ralph said. 'It's a beauty. We'll give it to Bill right in the forehead, same as the machete, but nobody can say we're ripping off *Friday Part II.* Bruce!'

'Yo,' the prop man called. He rushed forward, carrying a shiny new ax at port-arms. He handed it to Roger.

'Wicked, eh?' Roger winked behind his tinted glasses, and tapped a finger against the cutting edge.

'It's a bit too wicked,' Dani told him. 'It's a lot heavier than the machete, and the weight isn't distributed the same way.'

'Yes?'

'It would chop right through the catcher's mask.'

'Have your man pull the blow.'

She shook her head. 'He'd have to strike hard enough to penetrate the face appliance. It's too risky. Besides, it wouldn't look right. An ax just isn't a machete, Roger. It wouldn't go in

91

just a couple of inches. Not the way we'd want our maniac to swing it.' Dani drew a finger across her forehead. 'It'd pretty much take off everything from here up.'

Roger leered and nodded. 'Beautiful. That's what we'll do.'

'It'd take a full head appliance.'

'You'll have it ready for Monday?'

She nodded. 'Michael's about the same size as Bill. We can use his mannequin, attach Bill's head.

'Fine, fine. Go to it, kid.'

She explained the situation to Jack as they left the sound stage.

'That means we're done for the day,' he said.

'Yep.'

'Nice. If you want to bring the car around, Bruce and I can take care of Michael.'

'That's all right. I love to see all those old props. Like a museum.'

Bruce smiled over his shoulder as he unlocked the door. 'Just watch out for the mice,' he said.

'Mice?'

He laughed. 'Cute little critturs, but they have a tendency to get under foot.'

'I'll watch where I step,' Dani told him. In her boots and jeans, she felt well protected. Still, she spent most of her time studying the concrete floor as she followed Jack and Bruce through the narrow aisles.

On both sides, the warehouse was packed with furnishings. She saw a dusty, roll-top desk, highboys, dining room sets and sofas, floor lamps and table lamps and chandeliers. Then she watched the floor again, looking for mice but glancing at the framed paintings propped up on both sides of the aisle.

They turned a corner. She saw replicas of Venus and David, a statue of Napoleon, bird baths, fountains adorned with cherubs, naked women, a man balanced on one foot with his lips pursed to squirt.

She stepped on something small and soft. With a gasp, she jerked her foot up.

Only a scrap of thick-napped carpet.

'Here we are,' Bruce said.

Standing against the wall as if lined up for inspection were fifteen or twenty naked mannequins. Dani's eyes went directly to the life-like figure with the blasted face. Then she looked carefully up and down the row, pausing at each female.

She frowned.

'Where's Ingrid?'

'Ingrid?' Bruce asked.

'*Me*! Where is she?'

'Must be around,' he said.

'I don't see her,' Jack muttered.

Bruce shook his head, scratched his ear.

'You're in charge, aren't you?' Dani demanded.

'I put her there, right next to the fella. Had 'em both side by side.'

'She isn't there now.'

'I can see that, Miss Larson. Plenty of other folks have access here. Could be someone borrowed it.'

'I'd like to know.'

He scowled, looking puzzled. 'I'll sure look into it for you.'

Jack took her hand. 'I'm sure it'll turn up.'

'Yeah. Yeah, I suppose. I'm sorry, Bruce. I didn't mean to snap at you that way.'

'That's all right, Miss Larson.'

'I'm sure it's not your fault. It's just . . . I feel a certain attachment to the damn thing.'

'Well, I'll see if I can't turn it up.'

'Fine. Thank you. Now let's grab Michael,' she said, forcing cheer into her voice, 'and get this show on the road.'


Dani drove slowly past the guard station at the studio gate, and turned left onto Pico. She searched the rearview mirror.

No hearse.

Of course not.

'Jack?'

He looked at her.

'About Ingrid. You . . . you don't think there's any chance that Anthony got her?'

93

'*Anthony*?' He sounded shocked. 'No. How could he?'

'He might've sneaked onto the lot. It's not impossible. It happens.'

'Sometimes. But look, how would he know Ingrid has anything to do with you? She hasn't got a face, and I don't think Anthony's seen the rest of you well enough to recognise her other features.'

Dani blushed. 'If he was on the set Wednesday . . . '

'Did you see him?'

'No. But that doesn't mean he wasn't there.'

'He didn't *find* you until that night.'

'If he was telling the truth.'

'I imagine he was. Nothing happened before then.'

'He could've been at the studio, watched the scene with Ingrid, and *then* followed us to the restaurant.'

'I suppose. Why don't we ask him tomorrow?'

'Lot of good that would do.'

'Really, Dani, I don't think . . . '

'But what if he *does* have her?'

'Long as he hasn't got the real article,' Jack said. Reaching out, he rubbed the back of Dani's neck.

His hand felt good on her stiff muscles, but there was a cold knot in her stomach as she thought about Anthony with the mannequin.

Ingrid, but Dani.

She saw him in bed with her headless body, fondling her, kissing her, sliding a hand . . .

'Look out!'

She stood on the brake pedal. Her car shrieked to a halt inches from the rear of a van stopped at the traffic light.

'Are you okay?' Jack asked.

'Yeah. Fine.'

# FOURTEEN

CYNTHIA GABLE lifted her wine bottle toward the light and shook it. Through its tinted glass, she watched the cork toss like a tiny boat in a thrashing sea of Burgundy. She held the bottle steady. The tumult eased. The cork swayed back and forth, turning in a lazy way.

Murray had always been so good with corks. Plucked them right out. They never ended up in the bottom of the bottle when Murray did it.

Must be a trick to it.

Leaning over the coffee table, she stretched out her arm. The neck of the bottle hovered above her glass. She tried to hold it steady as she poured, but the bottle wavered. Some of the wine hit the rim and ran down the stem and made a shiny puddle on the table. Most of it, however, got into the glass.

She took a drink. A cool drop tapped her skin and trickled down between her breasts. She followed it with her finger, wiped it away, and licked her fingertip.

Least it missed the nightgown.

She licked the wet base of her glass, slid her tongue up its stem, up the rounded underside, found the rim again and drank some more.

Her eyes met the TV screen. Sandy Chung was on, doing a news break.

What happened to the show? Must be over.

What show had she been watching? Oh yes. *Dallas*.

Must be over.

She finished her wine. She set down her glass near the puddle, picked up the bottle and upended it. A few drops fell into her glass. The cork slid up the bottle as if to get out, but stopped when the neck narrowed and dropped back to the bottom as she put the bottle down.

95

A dead soldier. That's what Murray called them.

Not the cork, the bottle.

A dead soldier with a cork in his stomach.

The telephone rang.

Moaning, she pushed herself off the sofa. She swayed over the coffee table. As she raised her hands for balance, she saw herself in the mirror above the fireplace. The image looked at her as if she were a stranger. It raised its eyebrows, grinned in a crooked way, and waved a hand.

'Hiya, gorgeous,' she said, and winked.

The gal in the mirror winked, too.

'Scuse me, scuse me. Gotta get the phone.' She sidestepped past the coffee table. In the dark dining room, she grabbed the back of a chair to steady herself. With three long strides, she made it to the doorframe of the kitchen. She leaned a shoulder against it and lifted the wall phone's receiver. 'Hello?' she asked, pronouncing it carefully.

A low, breathy sound whispered in her ear.

'Hello?' she repeated the word.

'Shhuh . . . Shhh . . . ahhh.'

'That's easy for you to say,' she said, and a giggle slipped out. 'C'mon, who's this?'

'Ssss . . . Cynthia.'

'No, *I'm* Cynthia. Who's this?'

'Sssso cold.'

The low murmur of the voice sent a shiver up her back. She slid a hand down the wall and found the light switch. The kitchen went bright. 'I'm not in a mood for jokers,' she said.

'I . . . miss you . . . Cynthia.'

'You be'er tell me who this is.'

'Have you . . . forgotten me . . . so soon?'

She hung up. 'Jerk,' she muttered. She rubbed her arms. They were pebbly with goosebumps. Her nipples stood rigid against the soft lace of her negligee. She would put her robe on. That would be snug and nice. Then maybe another sip or two of wine.

She tugged open the refrigerator and took out a long, slim bottle of Chardonnay.

The phone rang again, making her jump. She snatched it off the hook. 'Hello?'

'Cynthia,' said the same, low voice.

'Who the hell *is* this?'

'I . . . I want you . . . with me. So dark here. So cold.'

'Who *is* this?'

'Mmm . . . mmmm . . . Murray.'

The bottle slipped from her hand. It thumped the floor but didn't break. It rolled a few inches and stopped. 'You're sick.'

'No, I'm dead.'

'You're a sick perverted bastard 'n I'm gonna call the cops.'

'Oh Cynthia, I'm so cold. I want your warmth. I want to make love with you.'

'You piece of shit!'

'I'm coming for you.'

She slammed the receiver down. Then she tugged at the phone, unplugging it. She rushed into her bedroom, flicked on the light, and dropped to her knees by the nightstand. She jerked the telephone plug from the wall.

There.

The bastard! The shit! What kind of animal would *do* such a thing? Nobody she knew. Must be a stranger, got her name from the obituaries. Maybe goes right down the list, calling every widow.

Sick!

*I want to make love to you.*

*I'm coming over.*

No, he won't come over.

Just a sicko gets his kicks with the phone.

She rolled onto her back on the soft carpet beside the bed. The ceiling turned slowly.

Go over to Barbara's?

But it's twenty minutes on the freeway. I can't drive. Not like this.

Call Barbara, ask her over?

Maybe.

He won't come. Those types never do. That's what the cops say on TV, and he always ends up coming. But that's TV. He won't come.

Just a harmless sicko.

Sicko. Revolting word, sicko.

And suddenly she knew she would throw up. Clutching her mouth, she staggered to her feet and ran for the master bathroom. Her stomach tossed. Her throat filled. She cupped her hands under her chin and tried to catch the hot flood and then she was at the toilet. She hunched over it, vomiting and sobbing.

When she was done, she cleaned herself off with toilet paper. She turned on the bathroom light. The top of her nightgown was clotted with mess. She wiped some of it off. She considered throwing away the gown, but Murray had given it to her last Valentine's Day.

She turned on the shower. When the water was as hot as she liked it, she climbed into the tub and pulled the curtain shut. The spray hit her face, patted her eyelids, filled her open mouth. It soaked her nightgown, making it cling in a way that felt good, almost erotic.

She used a soap bar on the soiled places. She rubbed it over her breasts until the fabric was sudsy and slick, then put the soap away and rinsed.

Bending over, she lifted her gown. She peeled it up her body and struggled out of it. She wrung the water from it. Then she opened the shower curtain and tossed it into the sink, and thought she heard the telephone.

Impossible. Just her imagination playing tricks.

A faint ringing sounded through the house.

Her bowels shriveled. She hunched low and shut off the faucets.

There it was again – a long, insistent ring that crawled up her body like the fingers of a dead man.

This can't be, she told herself.

Silence. She waited, hanging onto the faucet handles to steady herself, drops of cold water hitting the back of her neck.

It's stopped, she thought. Thank God it's . . . it came again, this time in a series of quick shrills unlike any noise her telephone had ever made.

The doorbell!

Someone's at the front door.

*I'm coming for you.*

But not Murray. The caller hadn't been Murray. He's dead.

The voice wasn't even his. Unless it had changed, somehow. Unless the accident . . . No, no, no. It was a sicko made those calls.

And now he's at the bell button.

He can't get in.

Maybe he can.

Maybe it's not him. Maybe it's Barbara or Louise or a neighbor or even the police.

Cynthia climbed out of the tub and ran, dripping, into her bedroom. She snagged her bathrobe off its closet hook. The ringing had stopped. Maybe *he'd* given up. Maybe he was making his way toward the back. But if it was a friend . . . She couldn't let a friend get away. Shoving her wet arms into the sleeves, she raced through the dining room. She pulled the robe shut and belted it.

In the living room, she grabbed an iron poker from the fireplace stand. She raced to the door. Her hand closed around the knob. The strength seemed to drain from her arm, from her whole body.

What if he's there, standing silent at the other side of the door, waiting?

Not Murray. It couldn't be Murray. He was in pieces from the accident, so even if . . . no, he's dead and in his grave and there's no way on God's earth it could be him.

It's the sicko who called, and he's standing just outside the door, no more than two feet away.

Cynthia's hand fell away from the knob. She stared at the door, wishing it had a peephole. But even if it did, she knew she couldn't bring herself to look out.

Water trickled down her legs, making the carpet wet around her feet. She swayed, taking deep breaths, and pressed a hand against her chest. Her heart pounded against it as if trying to smash through her ribs and escape.

*Go away!*

Maybe he's already gone.

I can't just stand here.

She gazed up at the guard chain. It was in place. She could open the door just a few inches, enough to look out.

No. No she couldn't.

But even as she told herself she didn't have the nerve, she saw her hand lift slowly toward the knob. Her numb fingers curled around it.

I can't do this!

She began to turn the knob and it pulsed against her palm as the door suddenly quaked. She jerked her hand away, lurched backwards. Blow after blow struck the door, shaking it in its frame.

Then it stopped.

'I . . . WANT . . . YOU!!!'

'No!' she shrieked. 'Go away!'

She heard the whisper of rushing footfalls.

He's leaving!

Somewhere outside, a heavy door thunked shut. A car engine sputtered to life.

Cynthia dropped her poker. She threw herself against the door, clawed the chain free and pulled the door open wide.

In her driveway stood a long, black hearse.

She shook her head, wanting to scream but feeling strangled. She stumbled forward one step. Her bare foot came down on something soft and crumbly. She raised it and grabbed the doorframe. In the porch light, she saw that the stoop was littered with fresh soil. Staggering backwards, she reached for the door.

She saw the hand.

Nailed to the outside of her door. A severed hand, filthy and blood-drenched. Red gore hung from the stump of its wrist.

She covered her mouth and screamed. The hearse sped backwards. She lunged into her house and screamed again as a glob dropped from the hand. She swung the door shut. Its bottom edge smeared the meat over her carpet.

Meat? It looked like ground beef. She crouched down for a closer look

Raw hamburger!

Gasping for breath, she jerked the door open again. The wrist of the nailed hand was hollow. She touched it.

Rubber.

A rubber hand.

She almost laughed, but she cried instead.

# FIFTEEN

LYING ON her side, Dani stared out at the sunlit pool. A beautiful summer morning. She listened to bird songs, heard the distant buzz of a power mower. The mild breeze carried a scent of grass and flowers. It felt cool on her bare shoulders. She pulled the sheet higher.

If only she hadn't asked Anthony to come over. The day could've been wonderful. Just she and Jack, lingering in bed, having breakfast by the pool, spending a few hours in the workshop, swimming later and relaxing in the sun.

Damn. That little invitation would end up ruining the day. She'd been an idiot to . . . no, it was the smart thing to do. Give the jerk what he wants, take the wind out of his sails. So far, at least, it seemed to be working; he hadn't bothered them since Thursday night.

He's probably staying home with Ingrid.

The thought made a chill creep up Dani's body. She rolled over. Jack was on his side, facing the other way. She snuggled against him, pressing her thighs to the backs of his legs, molding herself to the warm curves of his buttocks and back, kissing the nape of his neck.

'Mmm,' he said.

'Good morning.'

'Mmm. What time is it?'

'Eight.'

'So we have an hour before Terrible Tony arrives.'

'A whole hour.'

'Good. Just enough time for a swim, a shower, and breakfast.'

She slid her hand over his hip. Her fingertips brushed the coils of his pubic hair. 'Swim? I'd rather do something else.'

'Yeah?'
'Yeah.'


Dani lay on her back, arms and legs stretched out, letting the soft breeze cool her sweat. She felt used up and wonderful.

The shower made a quiet whispering sound like a wind in a forest.

She didn't have to move until Jack was through.

She glanced at the alarm clock. Twenty to nine. Just enough time for a quick shower and a cup of coffee before Anthony came.

Terrible Tony.

She smiled. Jack could be so serious sometimes, but his sense of humor was always lurking nearby, ready to spring out and surprise her.

The doorbell rang.

Her stomach tightened. 'Oh shit,' she muttered.

She looked at the clock. Eighteen minutes early. If it's him.

Sitting up, she used the sheet to dry herself. The bell rang again as she climbed off the bed. She stepped into her panties and white shorts, and pulled on her sleeveless sweatshirt as she hurried down the hall.

She opened the door.

'Greetings,' Anthony said. He held out a single, red rose.

'Why, thank you.'

He lowered his head. The ink eye had been washed off.

'Come on in, Anthony.'

He stepped into the foyer and looked both ways.

'Jack'll be along in a minute.'

'I knew he was here. I saw his car.'

'Would you like some coffee?'

'Does he live with you?'

'Yes,' she said without hesitation. It was none of his business, but she didn't want him to know that Jack might only be here on a temporary basis. She hoped it would become permanent, but . . .

'You're not married, are you?'

102

'No.'

'I didn't think so.'

'I'll put the coffee on.' She shut the door. Anthony followed her toward the kitchen. She felt uneasy walking ahead of him. 'Have you had any breakfast?' she asked, looking back at him.

'I don't eat it.'

'I'll heat up some bagels. You're welcome to join us.'

He sat at the kitchen table while Dani filled the coffee maker.

'Do you live near here?'

'Not far.'

'In an apartment?'

'I'll have a house in another year.'

'That'd be nice. Houses are nice. The prices are outlandish, though.'

'I'll be rich by then.'

'Well, I hope so.' She took bagels out of the freezer, unwrapped them and put them in the toaster oven. 'Do you work?'

'I'm the Chill Master.'

'I mean, how do you make a living?'

'I'm your assistant.'

Before Dani could find a response, Jack grinned at her from behind the bar. 'Been replaced already, have I?'

*Thank God,* she thought. Reinforcements.

Jack entered the kitchen. 'Hi there, Tony. A little early, aren't you?'

'Am I?' he asked, narrowing his eyes.

'I'd say so, yes. I barely had time to put on my face.'

Looking annoyed, Anthony turned to Dani. 'I think we should discuss the terms of my employment.'

'Nobody's mentioned employment,' Dani said.

'Just you, Tony.'

'What we talked about,' Dani explained, 'is showing you a little about how we work, getting you started in the right direction. Just as a favor.'

'You said you'd hire me.'

'No I didn't.'

'She didn't,' Jack said. He smiled at Dani. 'Shall we ask him to leave?'

103

She shook her head. 'Look, Anthony, I offered to help you. I think you probably have potential, but there are hundreds of people out there more qualified than you, people who've studied, who've worked long hard hours to develop their talents, and I'd be a complete jerk to hire you over one of them. Besides which, I already have an assistant.'

Jack nodded.

'But the offer's still open. If you want, you can spend the morning with us and we'll show you a few things.'

'Won't even charge tuition,' Jack added.

'We'll see how it goes today,' Dani said. 'If it works out all right, we'll discuss doing it again.'

Leaning back, Anthony folded his hands across the front of his black turtle-neck. 'I guess that's all right,' he said.

Dani poured the coffee. Jack carried two mugs to the table and sat down.

'Cream or sugar?' Dani asked.

Anthony shook his head.

Jack took a sip. 'So, tell me, scared the shit out of anyone lately?'

The boy grinned. 'Oh yes.'

'Want to tell us about it?'

Dani turned away to check on the bagels.

'I can't tell. I'm saving up all my tricks for my first feature.'

'Good idea. Keep 'em close to the vest. We Hollywood types love to steal hot ideas.'

'I know.'

'Should we let him in on our hot project?'

Dani shrugged.

'Oh, why not. The working title is *An American Were-oaf in Sardi's*.'

'Or *The Slobbering*,' Dani said.

'See, there's this guy . . .'

Anthony refused a bagel, but drank two cups of coffee while they ate. When they finished, Dani asked Jack to show him the workshop. She went into the bathroom, glad to be away from Anthony. She undressed and reached for the shower handle. Then she changed her mind. As much as she wanted to postpone returning, she knew it would be unfair to leave Jack alone with him for so long. She cleaned herself with a damp washcloth, brushed her teeth, and brushed the tangles out of her hair. Then she got dressed and headed for the workshop.

Jack and Anthony were at the far end, in front of a shelf lined with white plaster face molds.

'These are negative molds,' Jack said. 'We use them to cast positive molds out of celastic. That's a silicone rubber material. It's fairly rigid, but flexible, and . . . ' He stopped and smiled at Dani.

Anthony was smiling, too. He looked eager and happy. 'This stuff's great,' he said.

'Do you recognise any of the faces?'

He turned back to them, and shook his head. 'It's hard to tell.'

Dani stepped up beside him. 'This one's Adrienne Barbeau. Joe Spinell. Jamie Lee Curtis. This is Michael Fisher, who gets his head shot off in *Midnight Screams,* and the last one is me. I've got a small role in *Screams,* too. I also get my head blown off.'

'You're *in* the movie?'

'For about ten minutes,' she said, noticing his surprise. Was it an act? He must've known about her role, already, if he took Ingrid.

'This is Bill Washington,' Jack said, and lifted down both halves of the actor's mold. 'We have to make a prosthetic head of him for Monday.'

'Why don't we do a cast of Anthony's first?' Dani suggested. 'Would you like that?'

'Sure!'

'We'll give you the full treatment, and make a head for you at the same time we do Bill's. That way, you can see the whole process.'

They led Anthony to a straight-backed chair, and had him sit down.

'Would you like to be screaming?'

'That'd be great.'

'Okay. We'll do it with your mouth and eyes open.'

Jack turned on a gooseneck lamp and tipped it to shine on Anthony's face.

'You're not wearing contacts?'

'No.'

'You want to get the eyedrops and lenses, Jack?' While he went to the workbench, Dani explained the process. 'We'll be covering your head completely with alginade for the first impression. Any trouble with claustrophobia?'

'No.'

'Well, it only takes about three minutes to dry. It's a bit cold and uncomfortable, but it doesn't last long. We'll put in drops to anesthetize your eyes, and give you a couple of scleral contact lenses to protect them. Okay?'

'Sure,' he said, but his smile faltered.

For just a moment, Dani forgot all the trouble he'd caused. He was a teenaged boy, nervous and vulnerable, trying to be brave. She squeezed his shoulder gently. 'Don't worry, it won't hurt.'

He gazed up at her.

He no longer looked worried.

He looked adoring.

Dani let her hand drop. She wanted to take a step backwards, but Anthony's eyes held her like an embrace.

What have I done? she thought. My God, what have I done?

'Here we go,' Jack said.

His presence surprised her. 'Right,' she said, and felt as if she'd been snapped out of a trance. 'All set, Anthony?'

'I'm ready.'

'You put the eyedrops in, Jack. I'll get the alginade.'

The rest of the morning, she felt the difference in Anthony. The brief, sympathetic touch had changed him. He acted intensely interested in every detail of the work, but he studied Dani's face more often than he watched the procedures. He looked at her as if infatuated. The bitter sharpness was gone from his voice. He stood close to her, sometimes brushing her arm as if by accident.

While they were applying makeup to the finished heads, Anthony asked to use her bathroom. Dani told him where to find it, and he left.

'Want me to go out and keep an eye on him?' Jack asked.

'You can't very well do that.'

'He may do some snooping.'

'He had plenty of chance to do that the other day.'

'The other day, he wasn't so hung up on you.'

'Hung up?'

'Yeah. The kid's obviously fallen for you. I don't particularly blame him; you're easy to fall for.'

'Thanks.'

'But I don't much like the idea.'

'Neither do I.'

'What'll we do?'

'I don't know,' Dani said. 'It's a complication I hadn't counted on. I sure don't want to encourage him, but I don't want to dump on him, either.'

'Let's give him his head and send him home.'

'That won't be the end of it. As far as he's concerned, today's just the start. I think we'd be better off if we play along with him, ask him to come back but not till next Saturday.'

'I don't think he'll be happy about that.'

'We'll just explain that we're too busy during the week, and if he bugs us before Saturday, it's all off.'

'You're willing to have him as a permanent fixture on Saturdays?'

'Look, we can't just tell him to shove off. We'll be right back where we started.'

'When we started, he just wanted to get into special effects. Now, I think he wants you. It's only gonna get worse if we string him along.'

'Next, he'll want you.' Dani grinned, but Jack didn't.

'You've got it all wrong. He wants to *be* me.'

Dani felt a cold tremor in her stomach. 'Did you have to say that?'

'I didn't have to. You already knew it.'

The door from the kitchen opened, and Anthony came in.

Dani forced herself to smile at him. 'Well, I think we're about ready to wrap it up for today.'

'It's not even noon,' he said.

'We have some errands to run this afternoon.'

'I'll go with you.'

'No you won't,' Jack said.

Anthony stiffened and glared at him. He turned to Dani, his eyebrows lifting. '*You'll* let me come, won't you?'

'I think we should call it quits for today.'

'I won't be in the way.'

'Jack and I want to be alone.'

'Oh. What about tomorrow?'

'Tomorrow's Sunday.'

'That's all right.'

'We don't work on the Sabbath,' Jack said with a slight smirk.

'We have plans,' Dani said.

'Okay,' he muttered.

Jack picked up the duplicate of Anthony's head, and handed it to him.

'Come on by next Saturday,' Dani said, 'and we'll go over some more techniques.'

His lips peeled back as if he were in pain. '*Next Saturday*?'

'Same time, same station,' Jack said.

'That's *years*!'

'It's a week,' Jack said.

Dani opened the door, and they followed her into the kitchen. 'It'll be here sooner than you think.'

'I was thinking, you know, you'd take me to the studio and stuff.'

'I'd like to,' Dani lied, 'but it's against the rules.'

'You need a union card,' Jack added.

Anthony shook his head.

Dani led the way to the front door and opened it. 'I think it went really well today. You did a great job.'

'Yeah,' Jack said. 'Now you know how to make a decent head.' He tapped the nose of the head Anthony clutched under his arm. 'That's sure a far cry from the one you left on the diving board. Scarier, too.'

'Very funny.'

'If you have any spare time,' Dani said, 'drop by a library and pick up some books on cosmology, anatomy, that kind of thing.

108

They'll help. And we'll see you next Saturday at nine.'

'Okay. Well, thanks.' He stared at Dani's face as if to memorise it.

She smiled nervously. 'Bye, Anthony.'

He nodded, and turned away. He walked slowly toward the driveway, his head low.

Dani shut the door. 'Whew.'

'Alone at last.'

'I'm sweatin' like a huncher. Let's go for a swim.'

'What about those errands?'

'What errands?' she asked, and pulled off her sweatshirt.

# SIXTEEN

'No, HE'S not here just now,' said the woman's voice.

Linda eased the screen door open and peered into the house. A picture window filled the living room with sunlight. The woman wasn't there. Maybe in the kitchen.

'I don't expect him back for quite a while, Helen. He's off playing softball.'

Linda slipped inside. She inched the door shut.

'Certainly. I'll have him call you the minute he gets in. He's already told us all he knows, though. He hasn't seen Joel since Wednesday.'

Linda walked quietly to the staircase.

'He's as concerned as the rest of us . . . I know, I'd be a basket case, too. If I were you, I'd call the police.'

With a hand on the banister to steady herself, she climbed the stairs.

'No, I'm not suggesting anything of the sort, Helen. You're the one who's so sure he didn't just run away . . . I know he's not that kind of boy. That's why I think you should call the police. I wouldn't have waited *this* long, if it was Arnold.'

The woman's voice faded as Linda reached the top of the stairs. A door stood open to her left, another to her right. The corridor ran back alongside the stairwell with book shelves on the wall opposite the balustrade, and two doors near the end.

She glanced through the doorway on her right. A waist-high platform filled most of the room. An HO setup, complete with green hills, tunnels and bridges, a lake made of tinted glass, a little village with a train station. An assortment of miniature trains stood motionless on the tracks.

110

Across the hallway was a large bathroom.

Linda moved on. She heard footsteps below. With a glance over the railing, she assured herself that no one was on the stairs. She hurried toward the end of the corridor, and peeked into the room on her right.

A single bed. A cluttered desk and dresser. Plastic ship models on shelves. A poster of Reggie Jackson when he was still a Yankee.

It had to be Arnold's room.

Stepping inside, she quietly pressed the door shut. She went directly to the desk. On top were half a dozen school textbooks, a blue binder, scattered pens and pencils, a ruler, a gooseneck lamp, a pocket calcultor, a few loose paper clips, but no envelopes or stationery.

She lifted a straight-backed chair away from the desk and set it down gently. Then she slid open the top drawer. Near the front was a gum eraser, a compass, a sheath knife, a rubber mouse, a Kennedy half-dollar. To the rear, the drawer was heaped with papers, envelopes, and a few picture postcards.

With trembling fingers, she picked a glassy card off the pile. She stared at the grim, greenish face of the Frankenstein monster.

She flipped it over. The back was scrawled with pencil.


Howdy!
    Spent today at Universal Studios. Saw the old Bates house from Psycho. Castle Dracula was pretty neat, tho it didn't scare me any. You ought to get out hear.

So long.
C.M.


C.M.?

Linda would've bet the card came from Tony. Who the hell was C.M.?

Besides, it had no return address.

She dropped it, and picked up an envelope. In the corner was a return address written in shaky letters:

111

C.M.
8136 La Mar St. #210
Hollywood, CA 90038

Spreading open the envelope, she pulled out a folded sheet of paper. Strips hung off one side, like fringe where it had been torn from a spiral notebook. She opened it and read:

Howdy,

How're things in Dullsville? Just got me a place to live and a job all in the same day. Its part time at a Jack-in-the-Box. Where I work, not where I live. Ha ha!

Been seeing lots of movies. Theirs hundreds of theaters hear and some of them just show oldies all the time. Caught Chainsaw again last night. Its great hear.

Haven't run into Dick Smith or Rick Baker or any of those guys as of yet, but I hope to before to long. I'm going to be big, pal, just you wait and see. You can say you knew me way back when, or even better, you ought to come out hear and I'll get you in the movies.

So long from Hollywood.

Your pal,
The Chill Master

It *had* to be Tony.

C.M. Chill Master. What an asshole.

Linda folded the letter, slipped it back inside the envelope, and stuffed the envelope into the rear pocket of her shorts.

She heard voices. She heard footsteps. Arnold came into the room wearing sneakers, and sat on the bed to take them off. He dropped his soiled white socks. Standing, he lowered his jeans and shorts. He hopped out of them. He left them on the floor and walked to his closet. Then he went away.

Linda squirmed out from under the bed, pushing aside his shoes and socks. He'd left the door open. Keeping her eyes on it, she hurried to the closet. She slipped a plaid sports coat off its hanger and put it on backwards so it covered her T-shirt and shorts like a smock. Then she squeezed in behind the sliding doors.

She waited. Her heart pounded so hard it made her feel sick. Her tongue felt huge and rough in the dryness of her mouth. Sweat trickled down her face. She switched Arnold's knife to her other hand and wiped her slippery palm on the jacket.

Finally, he came back. The bedroom door latched shut.

Linda peered out at him.

His hair was wet and tangled. He took off a pale blue bathrobe and tossed it on his bed. He looked very muscular. His skin was tanned dark, his buttocks as white as loaves of unbaked bread. Squatting, he picked up his jeans. He dug into a pocket, came out with a comb, and dropped the jeans.

Linda eased her head out farther and watched him cross to the dresser. He stopped in front of it. Both hands went up, one combing while the other patted his hair in place. This would be a good time to go for him – except for the mirror. She drew her head in.

The comb made a quiet clatter. A few seconds passed. His quiet voice said, 'One . . . two . . . three . . .'

She looked again. Arnold was on the floor, hands clasped behind his head, sitting up. His back curled. He touched his elbows to his knees. 'Four,' he said, and lowered his back to the carpet. His penis, the size of a thumb, was pointed at the ceiling. His rising back blocked Linda's view. 'Five.' Down again.

She took a careful sidestep. Another. Now she was clear of the sliding door. She knelt.

'Eight,' Arnold said, and started down. His back pressed the carpet. He took a breath and gritted his teeth as if to hold it in. His stomach muscles flexed. His penis wobbled. He sat up, hands pulling at his head. Linda scuttled forward. Arnold's elbows brushed his slightly upraised knees. 'Nine.' He dropped back. His damp hair rubbed Linda's thighs, and she smiled down at him. His eyes opened wide. His mouth sprang open.

Linda thrust her open left hand against his mouth and leaned in, putting her weight on it, trapping his folded hands under his head and muffling his outcry as she swung her right arm down. The five-inch blade punched into him just above the navel. His knees

113

flew up. His hands escaped and reached for Linda's wrist but she jerked the knife out and raised it high. He tried to catch the blade. It stabbed his right palm, ripped open his forearm and plunged into his belly. The impact splashed blood high. It sprayed Linda's face. Arnold clutched her wrist. His hand was slippery and trembling, but his grip was strong enough to stop her from pulling out the knife. So she twisted it hard. He screamed into her left hand and his fingers fluttered open. She tugged the knife out.

His body was twisting and bucking, his arms flopping aimlessly, unable to stop her. She pounded the knife in. She found herself counting each time the hilt stopped her thrust. Eight, nine, ten, eleven. At twenty, she plunged the knife into his throat. She left it there, and rubbed off her fingerprints with the jacket.

She was exhausted. She got to her feet and pulled off the blood-soaked jacket. It had done its job well; there was not a drop on her own clothes. Using Arnold's bathrobe, she wiped blood from her thighs and knees, from her hands. It left them with a rusty stain. She turned to the mirror. Her face was speckled and dripping. Her wig, too. She cleaned them as well as she could.

Listening at the door, she heard nothing. She eased it open and checked the corridor. It was deserted. The sounds of a man and woman talking came from below.

She hurried to the bathroom. The air felt warm and moist. The top of the mirror was still fogged from Arnold's shower. She shut the door. Standing at the sink, she used soap and water to wash off the remaining bloodstains. She dried herself with a soft white towel.

Then she crept downstairs. The voices seemed to come from the kitchen. The living room was deserted. She eased open the screen door and stepped outside.

She crossed the lawn with her head down, rubbing her forehead to hide her face from any neighbor or passerby who might chance to see her. Once she reached the sidewalk, she let her hand down.

She noticed a kid across the street. He was hunched over the handlebars of his tricycle, pedaling furiously up his driveway. He didn't look back.

A car approached from the rear. She turned her head away until it passed, then scratched an eyebrow to shield her face from the rearview mirror.

At the end of the block, she walked around the corner to her parent's car. She climbed in. It felt like an oven. She winced as the vinyl upholstery scorched the backs of her legs, but smiled in spite of the pain when she heard the crumble of paper in her rear pocket.

Tony's letter.

With Tony's new address.

# SEVENTEEN

SWEAT AND suntan oil streamed down Dani's skin as she sat up. She stretched, enjoying the feel of the late afternoon breeze.

Jack, on the lounger a few feet away, seemed to be asleep. His hands were folded behind his head. His chest rose and fell slowly, skin glistening under his curly layer of hair. A puddle had formed in the depression of his navel. Its gleaming surface shimmered from the motion of his breathing.

Dani was tempted to go to him. He could use a little extra sleep, though, after spending so much of the past few nights awake. Restraining herself, she swung her feet down to the concrete and stood up. She walked silently, taking deep breaths of the breeze, trying to ignore the tickle of droplets skidding down her hot skin.

At the shallow end, she sat on the edge near the Jacuzzi and lowered her legs. She said 'oooh' as the water closed around her feet and calves. It was 80° F. but felt like the dregs of an ice bucket. After the first chill passed, she scooted forward and dropped into the waist-high water. She took a few steps, gritting her teeth as the bottom slanted down and the water climbed to her shoulders. An agony that she usually avoided by taking the cold shock in one quick dive from the side. But a dive might've disturbed Jack's sleep.

The things I'll do for him, she thought, and smiled.

In a moment, the water felt cool and pleasant. Letting her legs drift up, she did a silent breast-stroke. She neared the far end of the pool, started to make a wide turn, and saw Jack sit up.

'You're awake!'

'Who can sleep through all this splashing?'

'I didn't make a *sound*!'

116

He laughed softly. 'Actually, I haven't been asleep.'

'Not at all?'

'Not that I know of.'

'Humph!' Flinging up an arm, she caught an edge of the diving board. She raised herself enough to grab it with the other hand, and hung there, half out of the water, facing Jack. 'Come on in, I'll race you.'

'You always win.'

'You wouldn't want me holding back, would you?'

'It'd be the polite thing to do.'

'Want to tie one hand behind my back?'

'How about both?' he asked, and climbed off the lounge. He walked toward the diving board.

'I could drown,' Dani said.

'I'd save you.'

'You'd like that.'

'Likely.' The diving board wobbled as he walked out on it.

Dani swung herself sideways and clutched the end of the board with both hands. She hung on tightly as it shook.

Jack sat down, his legs dangling over the sides. Leaning forward, he looked down at Dani. 'You're beautiful when you're wet.'

'Thanks. What am I dry?'

'Ugly as sin.'

'Aren't you a charmer.'

His toes flicked against Dani's armpits.

With a yelp, she yanked herself up. 'You beast!' she cried.

Jack grinned.

Chin resting on the tip of the board, Dani bared her teeth at him.

He patted her head. 'Eaaasy, girl. Easy.'

'I'm gonna *get* you.'

'Oh, I hope so.'

'Can't tickle *me* and get away with it.'

'I'm not ticklish.'

'You'll be *sor*-ry,' she sang. Drawing her knees up toward the board, she tilted her head away and let go. Her back smashed the water. Blowing air out her nose, she kicked to the surface. 'Get you?'

'You're vicious!' he said, laughing as he raised his wet legs. 'That water's cold!' He got to his hands and knees, and peered down at her.

Lunging up, Dani grabbed the end of the board. She swung up her legs, hooked her feet over the edges, and pressed herself against its warm underside. She wrapped her arms over the top, and smiled at Jack. 'Even?' she asked.

'Even.' He lay down flat and kissed her. 'Something has come between us,' he said.

Dani nodded. 'I don't know about you, but I'm feeling board.'

He kissed her again.

'How about coming in now?' she asked.

He sighed as if frustrated. 'I'd like to, but I've got to get going.'

'*Going?*'

'I'm sorry. I meant to tell you sooner, but . . . hell, I really don't want to go.'

'Then don't.'

'I have to.'

'I've already got two lamb chops defrosted. I thought, you know, we'd barbeque them and . . . '

'It's a dinner engagement.'

'Oh.' She unhooked her feet, dropped into the water, and swam to the pool's edge. She boosted herself up. She walked across the concrete, leaving a wet trail, and sat down on her lounge. Picking up a towel, she began to dry herself.

Jack sat down facing her. 'I'm really sorry about this.'

'It's all right.' The towel was soft and comforting on her face. 'Who's the lucky . . . party?'

'No one you know.'

'Is it a she?'

'It's a she.'

'Your sister, I hope.'

'Methinks the lady's jealous.'

'Is it a *date*?'

Nodding, Jack leaned forward and braced his elbows on his knees. 'There is this other girl.'

'Oh man,' Dani muttered.

'Her name's Margot. She's a receptionist over at MGM. I met her there about a year ago, and we've been seeing each other on a fairly regular basis.'

'Is it . . . serious?'

'It's damn serious to her.'

'How about you?'

Jack knuckled a drop of sweat off his nose. 'A funny thing happened. I got a job working for this special lady and I wasn't so interested in Margot any more. First thing I knew, I was in love with this lady. She was my boss, though, so I kept it to myself and went on seeing Margot.'

His words warmed away Dani's dread. She moved over to his lounge and sat beside him. He rubbed the back of her neck.

'Anyway, all this with you came up pretty suddenly. The last Margot knew, she and I were still going together.'

'She doesn't know about me?'

'I haven't talked with her since Tuesday. That's when we made plans for tonight.' His hand roamed down Dani's back. 'Then, the next day, bang. Everything changed.'

'I didn't even know you *had* a girl friend.'

'She's probably going nuts wondering where I've been the past few days.'

'You should've called her.'

'I know. I'm not real handy at unpleasant chores. Besides, I figure it's only fair to let her know in person.'

'You're going to tell her about me tonight?'

'That's the plan.'

'That's awful.'

'Would you rather I didn't?'

'You'd better!'

'I will. I'll wait till after dinner, though. Don't want to ruin her appetite.'

'You'll come over afterwards?'

'It might be late.'

'I'll wait up.'

Dani kissed him good-bye at the door. 'Good luck,' she said.

He made a disgusted face. 'Why don't you come along?'

'Wouldn't *that* be charming.'

'Well, see you later.'

'You won't be too late?'

'I should be back by midnight at the latest. I hope.'

'Okay.'

He left. Dani shut the door. She started to hook the guard chain, but hesitated. If she fastened it, Jack wouldn't be able to let himself in.

I'll let him in, she thought, and pressed the disk into its slide.

Or maybe I won't.

Midnight. Dinner shouldn't take more than a couple of hours. Jack had said the reservations were for eight o'clock. What was he planning between ten and midnight? When *was* he planning to break the news? Right after dinner? Or right after . . . *One last time, for old time's sake.*

She felt disgusted with herself, imagining such a thing. Only a jerk would make love to a woman as a prelude to dumping her. Not Jack. But she could easily see him embracing her, consoling her after breaking the news, one thing leading to another, and maybe in the arms of this Margot he would decide not to give her up, after all.

The thoughts frightened Dani. She was leaning back against the door, breathing hard, her heart hammering, her mouth dry.

To lose Jack so soon . . .

What the hell am I thinking? It's the other girl who's getting dumped tonight, not me.

Poor girl. Christ, the poor damn girl.

Dani took a deep, trembling breath and pushed herself away from the door. She felt weak as she walked into the kitchen.

No good to dwell on that stuff.

Ninety per cent of worry is wasted effort, getting yourself all worked up over matters that never happen.

What about the other ten per cent?

Screw it.

*Please. Once more. For old time's sake.*

She looked at the kitchen clock. Just five. Seven hours till midnight.

I'll go to a movie, she decided. A double feature. Right after dinner.

It seemed like a good idea, and cheered her up. She took a glass from the cupboard, filled it with ice, and made herself a vodka and tonic.

Some women eat to cure their blues. Some buy new clothes. But Dani had found, over the years, that nothing worked better for her than a trip to the movies. It was an adventure. No matter how often she went or how rotten the films, it was always a treat.

Sipping her drink, she stepped around to the other side of the bar. She hopped onto a stool and opened the newspaper to the entertainment section. Her eyes roamed down the ads, seeking out familiar theatres.

She'd already seen most of the films playing nearby. Then she spotted a double bill playing in Culver City; *Zombie Invasion* and *Night Creeper*. She'd never heard of the first, but Larry Holden, a friend from her old job at EFX, had worked on *Night Creeper*.

She phoned the theater. With the next showing of *Zombie Invasion* at seven o'clock, she had two hours to eat, change, and get to the theater.

Setting down her glass, she stared across the kitchen at the two lamb chops she'd taken out for dinner. Her stomach fluttered at the reminder of Jack's absence, of his date with Margot. 'You guys thawed out yet?' she asked. She climbed off the bar stool and went to the counter. She poked one of the chops. Her finger dented the cool meat. 'Guess so.' They would save till tomorrow night, but she was hungry and she'd been looking forward to the lamb.

She put one into the refrigerator, picked up her drink as she passed the bar, and went out back. An hour and a half before time to leave gave her plenty of time to barbeque. She could shower and change while the coals heated.

She rolled her Weber grill away from the wall. Crouching, she opened the vents at the bottom of the drum. Ashes spilled out, dusting her hand. She brushed them off and removed the lid, then lifted out the blackened grill. The grate inside was scattered with powdery charcoal from last time. With tongs, she arranged

121

them into a pile. They would probably be sufficient for broiling one chop, but she didn't want to chance it so she hefted the bag of fresh briquets and dumped in some more. They tumbled and rolled down the heap of gray coals. Putting the bag aside, she used the tongs to set them back on the pile.

A match box was propped against the quart can of charcoal lighter. She picked up both. The can was heavy, almost full. She set the match box on the side tray and flipped open the red plastic cap of the fluid.

She squeezed out a long stream, waving it back and forth over the charcoals. It gave the fresh ones a shiny coat, turned the ashen ones black.

'Dani?'

Her hand jumped.

She tipped the can up and swung around.

He was at the side of the house, leaning in over the gate, a smile on his white, cadaverous face.

'Tony,' she muttered.

# EIGHTEEN

'WHAT ARE you doing?' he asked.

At a loss for words, Dani raised the can of charcoal lighter.

'Barbeque?'

She nodded.

'Can I talk to you?' Reaching over the redwood gate, he flicked up the latch. The gate swung open.

Dani licked her dry lips. 'You'd really better leave, Tony.'

He looked hurt. 'I won't get in your way. I promise. I just want to talk to you for a minute.'

He walked toward her. She nodded, trying to smile, well aware that she couldn't force him to go away.

His sunken eyes lowered, studying Dani as he approached.

Her striking bikini was one she never wore in public: a few wisps of filmy orange nylon held in place by knotted cords. She ached to cover herself, but didn't want Tony to know how vulnerable she felt. She set the fuel can on the tray. With effort, she resisted an urge to fold her arms over her breasts. She picked up her drink and took a sip.

'So, Tony . . . ' Her words sounded shaky. She took a deep breath and projected, her voice coming out firm. 'I thought we'd agreed on next Saturday.'

'I know. I'm really sorry to bother you. The thing is, I haven't made many friends since I've been here . . . '

Big surprise, Dani thought.

'And I didn't want to be alone. Not right now.' He looked at her with troubled, pleading eyes.

'Is something wrong?'

'I . . . I just found out my . . . my mother died.'

'Oh no. God, I'm sorry.' She stepped forward and took Tony's hand. She guided him to one of the lounges. 'Here, sit down.'

He lowered himself onto it and stared at the concrete.

'Let me get you something. A beer?'

'Okay.'

She rushed into the house, grabbed a can of Coors from the refrigerator, and hurried outside. Tony didn't look up as she lifted her own drink from the barbeque tray and walked over to him. She gave him the beer. She sat down, facing him. His bony fingers popped the tab, but he didn't take a drink. He turned the can slowly, staring at it.

'Had she been ill?' Dani asked.

He shook his head. 'It was very sudden. A heart attack. Dad said she was just standing there washing up the lunch dishes, and keeled over. She was dead by the time the ambulance arrived.' He shrugged again, and took a sip of beer.

'That's awful, Tony.'

'At least . . . it was over fast. I mean, that's better than a long illness, I guess.'

'Yeah,' Dani muttered. Her own parents were both alive, but she could easily imagine the devastation of losing one. She felt miserable for Tony. 'Were you very close to her?'

'We fought a lot. She didn't want me coming out here.'

'You're from New York?'

'Yeah. Claymore.'

'Will you be going back for the funeral?'

'I don't think so. Dad offered to pay my fare, but . . . what's the point?' He gazed at the top of his beer can, looking forlorn.

'Tell you what. Do you like lamb?'

'Sure.'

'It just so happens that I've got an extra lamb chop. How about staying for supper?'

'I don't think Jack would like that.'

'He won't be joining us.'

'He won't?' Tony frowned as if perplexed. 'Did something happen?'

'He's just got a previous engagement. He'll be back later.'

*By midnight.*

*Please. For old time's sake.*

124

'Why don't you go ahead and start the fire, Tony, while I get cleaned up a bit?'

'Start the fire?'

'Yeah. You know.'

'Maybe *you'd* better do that.'

'It's simple. All you've gotta do . . .'

'No, I can't. I'm sorry. I'll go away if you want, but I can't do that.'

'I'll start it.'

'I'm sorry.'

'That's all right.'

'I caught on fire once. That's why.' He pulled a leg of his black trousers up to his knee. The inner side of his calf was wrinkled and pink with scar tissue. 'See?'

'I'll start the fire,' Dani repeated.

He got up and followed her, but stood far back as she squirted more charcoal lighter onto the briquets.

She struck a match.

'Be careful,' Tony said.

'I'm an old hand at this,' she assured him, holding the flame to a coal. When that one caught, she moved the match to another and another until fire ringed the pile. 'That ought to do it.'

She picked up the grill and set it in place. The black grease on its bars hissed and smoked in the flapping blaze.

She turned to Tony. 'All set. Have another beer if you want. They're in the refrigerator. I'll be back in a few minutes.'

'Okay.'

Nodding, she turned away from him. She used the living room entrance, slid the screen door shut behind her, and left it unlocked so he could come in for beer.

She hoped that was all he would do.

Under the circumstances, she expected him to behave.

She couldn't trust him completely, though. When she shut herself inside the master bedroom, she snapped down the lock button. She closed the sliding glass door and locked it, then pulled the curtains.

Striding toward the bathroom, she saw herself in the full-length mirror – the orange bit of fabric hardly covering her pubic mound, the cord stretching around her bare hips to the brief triangle in back that left the sides of her buttocks exposed. My God, to think that she'd let Tony see her this way! And the top was no better.

The kid got an eyefull.

But at least he'd behaved himself. So far.

Hell, his mother had died. The last thing on his mind should be the state of Dani's undress.

Entering the bathroom, she pulled at the hanging strings of her bikini and slipped it off. She climbed into the tub.


Ten minutes later, dressed in top-siders, white jeans and a silken red aloha shirt, Dani left her room. She walked down the corridor, wondering if there would be time to prepare rice. That'd be cutting it close. Only an hour left before time to leave. Unless she wanted to forget about the movies. No. If she didn't go, how would she ever get rid of . . . Beside her, a door sprang open. She flinched, head snapping toward it.

Tony, just inside the guest bathroom, leaped back.

'Geez, Tony!'

He let out a nervous laugh. 'Startled me.'

'Yeah?' She pressed a hand to her throbbing chest and swallowed hard.

'I hope it was all right,' he said. 'I had to . . . you know.'

'That's what it's for.'

As he stepped out of the bathroom, the corridor seemed to shrink, trapping Dani close to him. She turned away. Her arm swept against the wall as she started forward. Tony stayed beside her. She felt suffocated, but forced herself not to rush. A few more steps. A few more. Then some of the oppression lifted, dispelled by the brightness and open spaces of the living room. She felt as if she could breathe again, but Tony's presence in the house still felt wrong.

He shouldn't be in here.

Not with Jack gone.

'Did you get some more beer?' she asked.

'Yes. Thank you.'

'Well, let's see how the charcoal's doing.'

Tony hurried across the living room and slid open the screen. As Dani stepped through, he moved forward and she brushed against him. She pretended not to notice. She felt relieved to get outside.

At the barbeque, she saw that the edges of the fresh briquets had turned gray. She lowered a hand close to the grill. There was heat, but not quite enough. 'I guess it's about ready,' she said. 'Would you like a salad?'

Tony shook his bald head.

'I'd make rice, but there really isn't enough time. I have to be going pretty soon.'

'Where are you going?'

'There's a couple of films I need to see.'

'You're going to the movies?' he asked, his small eyes opening wide. 'Can I go with you?'

Dani tried not to grimace.

'Please? I'll even buy the tickets.'

'There's no need for that.'

'I'd like to. Really. You've been so nice to me.'

'You've probably already seen the movies, anyway.'

'What are they?'

'*Zombie Invasion* and *Night Creeper*.'

'Wow! When did *they* open?'

'Yesterday, I think.'

'Man, I've really been looking forward to *Night Creeper*!'


Tony was eager to drive.

'No, that's all right,' Dani said as they left the house. 'We'll take my car.'

'Come on. It'll be fun. Have you ever gone in a hearse?'

'No. And it's an experience I plan to avoid as long as possible.' She smiled at her joke. Tony didn't. His mother had just died. Dani suddenly blushed at her tactless remark. 'Anyway,' she said, 'that monster must eat up gas like there's no tomorrow.'

'It is pretty bad,' he admitted.

Dani climbed into her Rabbit, leaned across the seat and

127

unlocked the passenger door. 'What ever possessed you to buy that thing?' she asked, passing it as she backed onto the road.

'It scares people.'

'Doesn't it scare you?'

'That's half the fun.' He turned in his seat to face her. 'It's fifty-two, you know. It was hauling stiffs more than ten years before I was even born. I figured it all out: if it even carried just two a week, that's more than three thousand in thirty years. was probably even more. Can you imagine all those bodies?'

'I'd rather not.'

'I've got a coffin in the back. A real nice mahogany one. Silk lining and everything. Sometimes, I sleep in it.'

'Wonderful.'

'Do you believe in ghosts?'

Dani shrugged.

'I do. Sometimes, I hear them when I'm driving.'

'Geez, Tony.'

'Moaning and groaning.'

'You're making that up.'

'No. Honest. And once, around midnight, a hand touched the back of my neck. I almost crashed. When I looked around, though, nobody was there.'

'Stop it, Tony. I'm serious. I don't want to hear this. If you keep it up, I'll turn the car around and that'll be it for the movies.'

'I just thought you'd be interested,' he said, sounding hurt.

'Some other time, all right?'

'Okay.' He sat forward and crossed his arms.

After a while, to break his gloomy silence, Dani asked about his favourite movies.

He immediately cheered up. '*Texas Chainsaw Massacre* is my all-time favorite.'

'Mine too.'

'Really?'

'Yep.'

'How'd you like it when he stuck that girl on the meat hook?'

'I cringed. I could almost feel it going in.'

'Yeah, me too. How about the old guy with the hammer?'

'Yuck.'

Dani found that she was enjoying their talk. As she drove down Crescent Heights toward Pico, they discussed Hooper's other works. The conversation shifted to films by Craven, Romero, Cronenberg, Carpenter. They talked about their favorite scene, Dani sometimes pointing out how certain effects were created.

'How about that shower scene in *Eyes of the Maniac*?'

'Oh, you saw that?'

'Four times,' Tony said. 'How'd you do that with the poker?'

'It actually penetrated a full body appliance we'd made up of Jenny – a dummy.'

'It looked so real.'

'Well, we made it from a cast of her. Basically the same technique we used on you this morning, except we covered her entire body.'

'Naked?'

'Yeah.' She thought of Ingrid.

'What were the guts?'

'Guts.'

'Real guts?'

'Pig entrails. We get them from a slaughter house.'

He shook his head. 'You do all that stuff, but you don't want hear about my death buggy.'

'That's right. I still don't.'

'What's the difference?'

'Films aren't real.'

'Pig guts are.'

'I don't enjoy that part. It's just necessary. Besides, I let Jack do most of the real grubby stuff.'

'It wouldn't bother *me*.'

'I'm sure. But anyway, that's the difference. Films are make-believe. Jenny Baylor didn't get skewered with a fireplace poker. After it was over, she went home. Not to a morgue.'

'But it scared the hell out of the audience. It grossed them out.'

'It's just toying with their imaginations. I mean, they let themselves believe the movie's real, but deep down they know it isn't.'

'So they aren't as scared.'

129

'They're *playing* at being scared.'

'That's why real life is better,' Tony said, and looked at her as if expecting a challenge.

'Skewering people?'

'No, scaring them. I've never hurt anybody. I just like to scare the shit out of them. Have you ever done that?'

'I've jumped out of the dark and yelled "Boo" a few times.'

'Isn't it a kick?'

'It's fun once in a while.'

'Doesn't it make you all shaky and excited. Hiding in the dark, just waiting to pounce?'

She shrugged.

'It turns *me* on.'

'Different strokes,' Dani muttered, and swung the car over to an empty stretch of curb. She glanced at her wristwatch. 'Five minutes to spare.'

Walking toward the ticket window, she opened her purse.

'I'll buy,' Tony said. He sounded determined.

Dani frowned. She doubted he had much money and she didn't want to fell obligated. On the other hand, a refusal might hurt his feelings. Men were usually strange that way. 'All right,' she said, and managed a smile. 'But you've gotta let me buy the popcorn.'

'A deal.'

My God, she thought, this is sounding like a date.

# NINETEEN

EACH CARRYING a tub of popcorn and a Coke, they made their way up a slanted corridor to the entrance of theater three. A sign above the door read 'ZOMBIE'.

For a Saturday night, the auditorium wasn't very crowded. They entered a row near the front, sidestepping past the knees of a teenaged couple.

'Here?' Tony asked.

Dani shook her head, not wanting to block the view of a black family already seated, though she felt a stir of anger at the parents. The baby in the woman's arms was probably too young to notice the violence and gore in these films, but the other two were older. They would notice, all right.

With a quick scan of the audience, she spotted at least fifteen other children. It wasn't unusual, but it never failed to sicken her.

They took seats as the theater lights dimmed. Opening her straw, Dani watched an ad for the *L. A. Times*. Then a trailer came on, warning the patrons not to flick their Bics 'in the thick of the flick'. It had seemed cute the first few times she'd seen it. She stabbed her straw through the slits of the Coke carton.

Tony's arm eased against her. She leaned sideways slightly to break the contact, and sipped her drink.

During the previews, a teenaged couple stepped into the next row. The boy sat down in front of Dani. For a moment, his head blocked the lower part of the screen. Then he leaned sideways, out of Dani's way, and put his arm around the girl in front of Tony. They whispered a few words. They kissed.

Dani felt a stir of longing. If only Jack were here . . .

*Zombie Invasion* started. The title flashed onto the screen, but there were no opening credits. They'd been edited out. A bad sign.

131

A young, dark-haired woman was strolling among cemetery monuments at night. She wore a long, white nightgown and carried a sprig of flowers. The scene looked familiar to Dani. As the woman knelt to place her flowers on a grave, a hand burst from the soil and grabbed her throat. It pulled her down. The breaking dirt spilled away, and a ragged, decomposing corpse rose up, its mouth agape to bite her.

*Did you catch that dental work on Stanley the stiff? Bleah! I don't know about you, boys and girls, but I'd rather kiss a toad. This guy is definitely not going to turn into a handsome prince.*

It was Livonia's sultry voice, as vivid as her amazing cleavage in Dani's mind. Livonia, the seductive vampire hostess of *Monster Matinee*. Sunday afternoons. Four o'clock. Channel six.

*Here's a gem you can really sink your teeth into . . . or fangs, as the case may be.*

'I'll be damned,' Dani muttered.

Tony leaned close, his arm once again touching her. 'Huh?'

'I saw this turkey on *television* last month.'

'Television?'

'It was called *Bite of Death*. Livonia showed it.'

'Really?'

'Distributor's shenanigans,' she said. She felt cheated and angry, then just disappointed. To have this happen on top of Jack's surprise date and Tony popping up . . . She sighed.

At least the afternoon had been nice.

Leaning away from Tony, she slumped down in her seat, crossed a foot over one knee and dug into her popcorn. She tried to watch the film. The dubbing was lousy, lips moving out of sync with the words. Even when the characters were outside, their voices reverberated as if recorded in a concrete room.

The story had been a bore the first time she saw it, made bearable only by commercial interruptions and Livonia's sarcastic comments. Watching it now, Dani entertained herself by recalling Livonia's quips and thinking up her own.

She and Jack would be trading remarks in soft whispers if he were here, having a great time, enjoying this dud. She realised, with some astonishment, that they'd seen no movies together since becoming lovers. They'd viewed dailies before, they'd gone to some screenings, but that had been part of the job. So far, they'd never sat in the darkness like kids on a date, holding hands and snuggling.

Maybe tomorrow night.

A drive-in. Fantastic! One of those in the valley. Pick a double feature they didn't really care about, because even if you're not fooling around you can't get that involved with a drive-in movie. And she planned to fool around. Definitely.

They should take a blanket alone.

She would wear a skirt.

As her mind lingered on the possibilities, she felt her skin heating, her heart speeding up, her nipples rising turgid against the caress of her shirt. The inseam of her jeans felt like a pressing hand.

Christ!

She sat up quickly to ease the pressure, and glanced at Tony, worried that he might somehow sense her arousal.

He turned toward her, eyebrows rising.

She forced a smile. 'How do you like it so far?'

'It stinks.'

'That's being generous.'

'I don't mind, though. I like being here.'

'Good. I'm glad.'

He stared at her. 'You were awfully nice to let me come along.'

'That's all right.' His gaze made Dani uncomfortable. She turned away. He kept on staring. She scraped up the last of her popcorn and ate it, watching the screen, trying to ignore him. She slipped a napkin from her shirt pocket. She wiped her hands, her mouth. She wadded it and dropped it into the tub. Tony's head was still turned toward her. She sipped the watery remains of her Coke, and finally looked at him. 'You're missing the movie.'

'You're so beautiful.'

His words made a cold place in Dani's stomach. 'Thank you,' she said.

A smile trembled on Tony's lips and he turned away.

Dani took a few slow, deep breaths to calm herself. Then she bent down and placed her empty containers on the floor. She sat up. Her shoulders pressed Tony's outstretched arm. She flinched as its touch, but forced herself not to lurch forward.

'Please, Tony.'

'Did I startle you?' He rubbed her right shoulder, making the silken shirt slide against her skin.

'We're not here for that. Please.'

'Why?'

'I *have* a boy friend.'

'You mean Jack?' The hand continued to caress her.

'Yes.'

'He's not here.'

'That's not the point. Take your arm away.'

It stayed. 'Don't you like me?'

'Tony!'

It lifted, swung over her head, and settled on the armrest between them.

'Thank you.'

'I didn't mean any harm,' he said, sounding pitiful.

'I know.'

The boy in front of Dani looked back and frowned. 'Sorry,' she whispered. Turning back, he snuggled down again with his girl friend.

Tony crossed his arms and stared at the screen.

'It's all right,' Dani whispered. 'Don't feel bad.'

He nodded slightly, but didn't look at her. He blinked. Tears spilled from the corners of his eyes, making shiny streaks down his face. He sniffed and wiped them away.

Reaching out, Dani patted his knee.

He gazed down at her hand. She turned it over. Tony's hand pressed against it. She closed her fingers and squeezed gently. 'Friends?' she asked.

'Yeah.'

She held him for a moment. With a final squeeze, she let go and folded her hands on her lap. Bringing him to the movies had been a great mistake. She should've known better. She'd been pushed into it, but she could have refused. A simple no. Instead of that, she'd let her sympathy get in the way and twist her perspective.

She felt a stir of anger. At herself. At Tony. He'd used his mother's death as a lever to force his way deeper into her life. It wasn't fair.

She should've listened to Jack's advice at the outset: don't feed it, maybe it'll go away.

And what does she do? She feeds it. Brilliant move. A little kindness goes a long way. Now this weird kid thinks he's her boy friend.

And she feels like a jerk for upsetting him.

Just wonderful.

On the screen, a horde of grisly corpses was rampaging through an apartment complex, bashing down doors, dragging their hysterical victims from hiding places in closets and bathrooms, under beds, ripping off arms and legs, devouring flesh.

Not exactly Livonia's version. Most of the gore had been edited out for television.

A cut to the room of Elizabeth, the heroine. She was busy shoving a bureau against her door, not knowing that one of the zombies lurked inside her bathroom.

Almost over. Dani felt a tremor of dread. At intermission, she would have to face Tony in the light. What the hell would she say to him?

Tell him you have to use the restroom, and stay there till the next film starts.

That's a chicken way out.

The zombie swung open the bathroom door. He staggered toward Elizabeth. She was leaning forward against the bureau, unaware of his approach.

Lousy makeup on the zombie. It looked like a Halloween mask. The audience sounded frightened in spite of it.

Only a couple of minutes before intermission. Dani wiped her sweaty hands on her jeans.

Just explain, as gently as possible, that you appreciate his friendship . . .

The zombie reached out, his decomposing fingers only inches from the back of Elizabeth's neck.

You're flattered that he finds you attractive, but . . .

Tony sprang forward, growling, baring his plastic fangs, clutching the neck of the girl in front of him.

# TWENTY

THE GIRL shrieked.

Elizabeth shrieked.

The audience erupted with cries of fright and alarm. The boy friend whirled around. Dani grabbed one of Tony's arms and tugged it away from the girl. 'Let go!' she snapped. He tried to jerk free, but she held on tight until the boy flung himself over the back of the seat.

The boy fell across Dani, knees digging into her thighs, elbow jabbing her cheek as he clambered over her. He hooked an arm around Tony's head. He twisted it, squirming on Dani, grunting each time he struck. Though she shoved at him, it seemed to have no effect. His fist thudded against Tony. He pounded very fast and very hard, as if he knew he didn't have much time. A horrible, gasping whine came from Tony.

'Stop!' Dani cried.

She dug her fingers into the boy's thick, greasy hair and yanked with all her strength. His head flew back and his body followed, his weight crushing Dani as he swayed, kneeling on her lap. She thrust against him. He fell sideways against his own seat back, crying out as the edge caught his ribs.

The theater lights came on.

The boy tried to untangle his legs from Dani's. She kicked at him until he managed to throw himself over the seat.

A husky, bearded man in a necktie grabbed the boy roughly and jerked him upright. 'Get out of here!'

'But . . . '

'Get! Don't let me catch you in here again!'

Muttering curses and glaring at Tony, the boy followed his girl friend down the row. At the aisle, he turned around. 'Crazy fuckin' maniac!'

With those two leaving, everyone in the theater seemed to be gaping at Dani and the man.

'You too,' he snapped. 'Out of here!'

For the first time since the assault, she looked at Tony. He was sprawled crooked, half off his seat, arms and legs at strange angles that made Dani think of broken spiders. He was panting hard. His head hung to one side. Blood spilled from his open mouth, his split lips, his nostrils, gashes and a few scratches apparently made by a signet ring. One eye was nearly swollen shut.

Dani gazed at the damage, appalled. A minute ago, Tony's face had been intact. Now it looked worse than some of her makeup effects. But this wasn't makeup; the red stuff wasn't a sweet mix of Karo syrup. This was mauled flesh and real blood.

Looking at him, she felt sick and helpless.

'Come on, sister, move it. You're not outa here in two minutes, I'm calling the cops.'

She grabbed one of Tony's hands and pulled, but only managed to swivel him sideways a bit.

'All right,' the man said, sounding disgusted. 'Move aside. I'll get him.'

'Thank you,' Dani said. As she waited for him to come around the end of the row, someone tapped her shoulder. She turned. A teenaged boy squinted at her through thick glasses.

'You *are* her, aren't you?'

'Huh?'

Shaking his head in disbelief, he reached into a side pocket of a sports jacket too small for his girth and pulled out a Gary Brandner paperback. 'I'm a great admirer of your work, Miss Larson. I wonder if I might trouble you for your autograph.'

'Sure.' She glanced back. The man was pulling Tony out of the seat.

The boy ripped out a page and gave it to her along with the book and a pen.

'Make it to Milton,' he said.

She started to write. Her hand trembled.

'Come on, sister,' the man called from behind.

She continued to write, burning with embarrassment. She'd

never been asked for an autograph before. She wished it hadn't happened now.

'I'm really into makeup, myself,' Milton said.

'I'm glad to hear it,' she managed. She gave back the page, the book and pen, then held out her hand. Looking surprised, he shook it. 'Good luck to you, Milton.'

He nodded and blinked and turned red. 'I hope you're not in any trouble,' he said.

'Thanks. I'll survive, I guess.' Then she turned away and hurried up the row.

By the time they reached the lobby, Tony was walking under his own power.

'I'm awfully sorry about this,' she told the man.

'Just keep your boy friend away from here.'

'He's not . . . ' Why bother? 'Yes sir,' she said.

He held the door open, and she hurried outside ahead of Tony. Near the curb, she waited for him to catch up.

'Geez, Tony.'

'You mad at me?' His words were fuzzy and distorted as if he had a bad cold.

'Oh, why should I be mad? I haven't had such fun in ages. It's great sport getting pounded, humiliated, and thrown out.'

Tony frowned and winced. 'Did he hurt you?'

'Not as much as he hurt you, obviously.'

They started walking. Tony moved slowly and stiffly, as if careful not to jostle himself.

'We'd better take you to emergency,' Dani said.

'No. I'm all right.'

'You look all right.'

He touched his face with both hands, exploring the damage. 'He got me pretty good. Think I'll have scars?'

'More than likely.'

'I hope so,' he said, and walked into a parking meter. He bounced off, crying out and staggering sideways. Dani braced herself against his impact. His shoulder bumped her chest and knocked her backwards a few steps. She threw her arms around him, holding him up.

'God, Tony.'

He moaned.

'Come on.' Hugging his arm, she helped him straighten up. They started walking. His upper arm was pressed tight against her breast. She suspected that he was very aware of it, in spite of his condition. She eased away just enough to get his arm off her breast, but continued to grip him with both hands until they reached the car. He leaned against it while she opened the rear door. Then she helped him in. He lay on his back and drew his knees up.

As she drove, Dani considered taking him to an emergency room. He didn't want that, though, and his injuries did seem superficial. Besides, she couldn't just drop him off and leave. He would need transportation back to her house.

Give him the taxi fare.

No, she couldn't do that. She'd have to wait with him, and she hated hospitals.

'Boy,' he said from the back seat. 'Did you hear that gal scream?'

'I heard.'

'She probably wet her pants.'

'Tony'

'I really got her, huh?'

'I hope it was worth it.'

'It was great.'

'Don't you ever worry about the consequences of your little escapades?'

'Huh?'

'You not only got us both hurt and kicked out, you probably frightened that poor girl half to death.'

'Yeah,' he said, sounding pleased.

'It's nothing to be proud of. Besides, you ruined the end of the movie for everyone in the theater.'

'It was a crummy movie.'

'The people still . . .'

'And even if it wasn't, I mean, I gave everyone there a thrill they'll never forget. You know? I gave 'em more than a movie. Something to tell their friends about. Boy, every time they go to a movie, they'll remember what I did tonight.'

'Hooray for you.'

'I'm sorry *you* got hurt.'

'You should've thought of that before you attacked that poor girl.'

'Yeah. I'm sorry. Honest, I wouldn't have done it if I'd known.'

Dani said nothing.

Tony was silent for a long time. Then he said, 'I'm sorry' again, this time in a shaky voice. She heard him sniff.

He's crying again.

Dani sighed, feeling sorry for him in spite of everything. Christ, he'd lost his mother today, his romantic advances had met a rebuff, he'd been pounded into a bloody mess, even crashed into the damn parking meter. Matters couldn't go much worse for a kid.

He'd brought much of it on himself, but Dani had contributed to his misery.

He lay quiet, sniffing occasionally, until they were on Laurel Canyon. 'Are we . . . almost there?'

'Just about.'

'I guess you don't want to see me again.'

Here's your chance, Dani thought. Say 'That's right,' and it's over. Maybe. But she couldn't do it to him. 'If you think you can behave, you're welcome to come back next Saturday like we planned.'

'Honest?'

'Yeah.'

'Why . . . how come you're so nice to me?'

''Cause you're so sweet.'

He laughed, but it sounded close to a sob.

Approaching her house, Dani saw the hearse parked in front. She hoped to find Jack's Mustang in her driveway, but wasn't surprised when it wasn't there. Only about nine o'clock. He and his Margot were probably right in the middle of their main course.

She parked to the side, leaving room for Jack's car, and climbed out. She opened the rear door for Tony. He stood up, hanging onto it for support.

'Are you all right?'

'I guess.'

'You think you can drive okay?'

140

He shrugged, grimacing as if the movement hurt. 'I . . . I'm awfully thirsty. Maybe . . . could I use your garden hose?'

'That's not necessary. Come on.' They walked toward the front door, Tony with his arms pressed to his body as if holding himself together. 'You might as well fix yourself up while you're here. Get some disinfectant on those wounds.'

'I don't want to be any trouble.'

'It's no trouble,' she said, opening the door. Remembering her boxed-in feeling earlier, she hurried down the corridor ahead of him. She turned on the bathroom light. Tony entered as she took iodine and a canister of bandages from the medicine cabinet. She set them on the counter. She plucked a cardboard cup from a wall dispenser and gave it to him. His hand was rust-brown with drying blood.

He thanked her.

'You go ahead and patch yourself up.'

'Where are you going?'

'Just in the kitchen.'

'Do you have to go?'

'I think you can handle this by yourself, Tony.'

He made a disappointed sigh, but Dani didn't give in. Already, she felt nervous being in the bathroom with him. If she stayed, he would ask her to help clean him, bandage his wounds.

No way.

'Excuse me,' she said.

He made no attempt to stop her.

The kid's shaping up, she told herself as she stepped into the corridor.

She poured a vodka and tonic, and swung herself onto a stool along the short side to the bar. From there, she could see the length of the corridor. The bathroom door stood open. She heard water running. She assumed he was still in there. But . . .

In her mind, she saw him sneaking out, hurrying to her bedroom while she was busy making her drink, undressing . . . Don't be absurd.

Still, it had probably been a mistake to let him come in. The kid's unpredictable.

The water shut off.

At least he hadn't left the bathroom.

What if he *does* try something?

Dani took a long drink and set her glass down. Her gaze lifted to the counter across the lighted kitchen, lingered on the rack of butcher knives.

Now who's the crazy one?

With a shake of her head, she lifted her glass and drank.


She was leaning against the bar counter about to sip her second vodka and tonic when Tony stepped out of the bathroom. 'All fixed?' she asked.

He nodded.

Setting down her glass, she pushed herself away from the bar and walked toward him. She felt calm, a bit light-headed. The double shot of vodka in the first drink had worked wonders on her nerves.

She stopped in the foyer.

He walked toward her stiffly, hunched over a bit, his head low, his arms straight at his sides.

'Do you feel like there might be internal injuries?' Dani asked.

'I don't know.'

'There was blood in your mouth.'

'It's cut up inside. I bit my tongue, too.'

'That'll teach you to go around scaring people.'

He raised his head and appeared to smile, though his swollen lips barely moved. His face was a patch-work of bandages, puffy and discoloured. His left eye looked very bad. He seemed to be gazing at Dani through a gash in an oyster.

'Can you see all right?'

'Yeah.'

Reaching for the doorknob, she felt her heart speed up.

Please, she thought.

She pulled open the door. 'Well, be real careful driving home.'

He stared at her. His right eye blinking. 'I'm not sure I can drive.'

'Give it a try.'

He nodded. 'Guess you want to get rid of me, huh?'

'It's been a long day. I'm really tired.'

'Yeah.'

'Goodnight, Tony.'

He stepped into the doorway and turned to face her. 'I'll see you next Saturday?'

'Right. Nine o'clock.'

He took a deep breath, and sighed. 'I'm sorry I messed up. I . . . I like you a lot, Dani. A real lot. I don't want you to hate me.'

'I don't hate you, Tony.' Reaching out, she squeezed his forearm. 'Take it easy, now.'

'Yeah. You too.' He turned away.

Dani stood with a hand on the door until he was gone. Then she swung the door shut, locked it and fastened the chain. She went into the kitchen, turning off its light as she passed. At the window, she watched Tony's dark figure move slowly down the driveway.

She waited. The tail lights came on. Then the hearse pulled forward and vanished. The street was a dead end. She didn't leave the window until the long, black car sped by, heading out.

Then she stepped over to the counter. Lifting the tail of her shirt, she slid the carving knife out of her rear pocket.

# TWENTY-ONE

HE PARKED in the car port. Climbing out, he crouched by the open door. He reached under the seat and slipped out a towel-wrapped object. He held it against his belly with both hands, and walked carefully to the apartment house entrance.

If he stumbled, if he dropped it . . . The towel would cushion its impact, but probably not enough.

Shouldering open a swinging glass door, he entered the lighted foyer. He made his way up the stairs to the second floor. The hallway stretched before him, dark except for a ceiling light near the far end. Normally, he didn't mind the gloom. Tonight, it worried him. If he tripped over something . . . just be careful, very careful.

At last, he reached his door. He cradled the bundle in one arm, and pushed his key into the lock. The door opened on darkness. He stepped inside, and wished he'd left some windows open. The room was stuffy and hot, almost smothering.

He found the light switch. A lamp came on, throwing its dim glow on the sofa, on movie posters tacked along the wall. The sofa creaked as he sat down under his *Eyes of the Maniac* poster.

He rested the bundle on his lap. With trembling hands, he folded open the towel. He stared at the white, plaster mask. The features looked only vaguely familiar. For a moment, he wondered if, in his rush, he had somehow taken the wrong mask from the workroom. He lifted it toward the lamp, studied it more closely. No, he'd made no mistake. This was Dani, all right.

His fingers caressed the cool, hard contours of her face.

Then he carried the mold to the table in his kitchen nook. He set it down carefully. Stepping around the table, he slid open a window. A slight breeze cooled the sweat on his face. He took

144

off his shirt, stood there feeling the breeze against his skin, then turned away.

In his bedroom, he sat on the edge of the mattress and gazed into the open closet as he pulled off his shoes and socks. All but her legs were hidden behind the hanging clothes.

Stripped down to his shorts, he went to the closet and slid the hangers aside. 'Peekaboo,' he said. Hands under its armpits, he lifted the headless dummy out of the closet.

'Miss me?'

He kissed the smooth latex skin of its belly.

'I brought you a present, honey.'

He kissed a jutting nipple, felt a stir in his groin, and set the dummy down.

'I can't tell you, it's a surprise.

'A hint?

'Let me think. It's something you need very badly if you want to get ahead.'

# TWENTY-TWO

TEN MINUTES before midnight, Jack arrived. Dani unchained the door for him. The throat of his sport shirt was unbuttoned, his necktie askew. Gripping the tie, she pulled him close and kissed him. He seemed tense. Dani's stomach tightened.

'Well,' she said. 'How'd it . . . '

'What happened?' Frowning, he brushed a fingertip over her sore cheek.

'Tell you later. Come on, I've got a surprise for you.'

She took his hand and led him toward the bedroom. 'How was dinner?'

'The pits. I didn't have much appetite.'

'You told her?'

'Yeah.'

'How'd she take it?'

'Not good.'

'I'm sorry.'

'She just wouldn't stop crying.'

'Where did you tell her? At the restaurant?'

'At her place. After dinner.' He shook his head. 'God, it was awful. It made me feel like such a bastard.'

'This'll make you feel better,' Dani said, leading him across the bedroom. She slid open the glass door and stepped outside. The overhead lights were off. The pool shimmered pale blue. The Jacuzzi at its near corner bubbled red like a cauldron. Towels were stacked beside it. A pair of wine glasses stood alongside the ice bucket. The neck of a bottle protruded from the ice.

'I don't believe it,' Jack said.

Turning to him, Dani opened her robe and let it fall away. She tugged at his necktie.

He was smiling, shaking his head. 'You're pretty fantastic, you know that?'

'I figure you had a rough night.' She dropped the tie and began to unfasten his shirt, her hands fumbling with the buttons as he stroked her breasts. When the last button was open, she unbuckled his belt. She unhooked the waist, lowered the zipper, and drew down his slacks and shorts. Smiling up at him, she lightly squeezed his scrotum. Her fingers curled around his erect penis, moved up it. 'Did you save yourself for me?' The words seemed to slip out, shocking her.

Jack laughed. 'It weren't easy, babe. I had to fight her off.'

'Really?'

'Yeah, as a matter of fact. She wanted one to remember me by.'

'Did she say that?'

'Not exactly. I don't know. Maybe she thought it'd change my mind.'

'Maybe it would've.'

'I didn't stick around to find out.'

'I'm glad. It would've been lonely in the Jacuzzi.' She leaned into him for a brief kiss, stroking his back, rubbing herself against the soft hair of his chest, feeling his hardness against her belly. 'I feel sorry for her, though.'

'And guilty?'

'A little.'

'Don't. I would've broken up with her anyway. I knew I didn't love her. Even before I met you, I knew that.' He kissed the tip of Dani's nose. 'I *do* love you.'

She hugged him tightly, her eyes suddenly filling with tears. 'I . . . I love you, too.'

For a long time, they held each other and didn't speak. Dani felt very strange: comfortable, lazy, excited, out of focus. Though she'd been sure Jack loved her, his words somehow made it different. She felt close to him as she never had before. 'Guess this calls for a celebration.'

'Well, you've got the right fixin's.'

They climbed down into the spa. Standing in the waist-high

swirl of hot water, Dani filled the wine glasses. She handed one to Jack, and sat beside him. 'To us,' she said.

'You and me, babe.'

They clinked their glasses, and drank. Dani scooted down a bit. The seething water wrapped over her shoulders. She felt Jack's hand on her thigh.

'Now,' he said, 'tell me about your face.'

She stared down at the red light near her feet, and took a deep breath. 'A guy . . . he roughed me up a bit at the movies.'

'You went to the movies? Alone?'

'Not alone.'

'Oh?'

'Tony came by.'

The fingers tightened on her leg.

'I didn't know what to do, Jack. He was feeling real down. He'd just found out his mother had died.'

'He came over to cry on your shoulder?'

'Apparently, he doesn't have any other friends.'

'That hardly comes as a surprise.'

'I felt sorry for him. You would've, too, if you'd been here.'

'He must've known I was gone. What time did he show up?'

'A little after five.'

'Just after I left? The bastard was probably watching the house. What ever possessed you to let him in?'

'He sort of let himself in. I was out here. He came through the gate.'

'My God, the nerve of that kid.'

'It's all right, Jack.'

'He didn't try anything funny?'

'He behaved himself fine. At least till we were in the movies.' She told about Tony grabbing the girl, about the boy friend scrambling onto her and pounding Tony, about getting kicked out of the theater.

'At least the jerk got what was coming to him,' Jack said.

'He was really messed up.'

'Good. He deserved it. About time somebody laid into him. I wouldn't mind doing it myself. Christ, he comes sneaking by the first time I'm gone . . . '

'He needed someone, Jack.'

'Yeah. You.'

'He'd just lost his mother.'

'Mighty good timing on the old gal's part.'

Dani turned to Jack. He took a sip of wine and met her gaze. Under the water, his hand stroked her thigh.

'You think I'm pretty callous, huh?'

'I know better. It's just that you've got this thing about Tony.'

'Yeah, this thing. He scares me. He's a sneak and a lunatic and he wants you. What'll he do the next time you're alone? Wait, don't tell me. Let me guess. His father has just passed away, and he's oh so sad . . . '

'Jack!'

'I'm sorry, but from what I've seen of our friend Tony, I'd bet a month's salary that his mother didn't die today. He made it up to get your sympathy.'

'Nobody'd do that.'

'Tony would.'

She stared at Jack, all the evening's events rushing through her mind. She felt dazed at first, then outraged. She knew that he was right. Tony had lied, used her sympathy like a weapon to force his way in. 'How could he *do* that to me?'

'Because, my dear, he's a slimy bastard.'

'He's had it.'

Jack patted her leg. Then his arm lifted out of the water and lowered behind her shoulders. He held her close against him. 'Time to rethink our position on Tony.'

'I don't want to see him again.'

'Next time he shows up, I'll point that out to him.'

'The dirty little shit.'

'On the other hand, maybe his mother *did* die today.'

'Sure,' Dani muttered. 'I'll believe that when I see the death certificate.'

# TWENTY-THREE

DEAR MOM, and Bob,

Please don't worry about me. I'm all right. I can't stand it with these murders, however. I may just be paranoid, but I knew Joel and Arnold and I keep thinking, who knows, maybe I might be next. It's just a feeling I have, but I don't mind telling you I'm scared.

If the murderer wants to kill me, he will have to find me first.

I hope you don't mind, but I borrowed your 'emergency money' in the dresser. I promise I'll pay it back when I can. I also drew out the baby-sitting money from my bank account. It's not a lot, but it will get me by until I find a job.

Don't worry about your car, Dad. I'm the one who took it. I will send a letter, soon, and let you know where to find it. I'll include the parking lot ticket.

I am very sorry about this. I promise to keep in touch, and I will return as soon as the police rid our town of its homicidal maniac.

Love always,
Linda

She placed the note on her parents' dresser, then opened the third drawer from the top. The stack of twenty-dollar bills was hidden between two neatly folded sweaters, just where it had always been. She counted. There were ten bills.

She found her father's Smith and Wesson on his closet shelf. She stuffed it into her overnight bag and closed the zipper.

It took nearly half an hour to walk to the Big Ten grocery store managed by her father. Along the way, she ran into Ginger Jones. The chubby old lady greeted her like a dear friend. 'Don't you look pretty, now? Where would a girl be going, all dressed up to the hilt that way?'

'I'm meeting Dad at the store. He's taking me in to Buffalo to visit my Aunt Vivian.'

'Well, you give Vi my regards, won't you?'

'I sure will.'

In the store's parking lot, she made a quick scan to look for her father. He wasn't in sight. She climbed into his car, and drove to the bank.

The clerk gave her no trouble. She added $185.63 to her bill fold.

Then she drove out to US 81. An hour and a half later, she took a parking lot ticket from a machine at Syracuse's Hancock International Airport. She carefully marked the car's location on the ticket before walking to the terminal.

The moment she stepped inside the terminal, panic hit her.

*I don't know what I'm doing!*

She staggered back a step. Still time to get home, tear up the note . . .

No!

She looked at the long counter, the ticket agents.

What's the big deal? All I've gotta do is buy a ticket. People must do it all the time.

How the hell do you do it?

Walk up to the counter. That's all it takes.

She walked up to a counter. A young man in a TWA blazer smiled at her. 'May I help you?' He raised his eyebrows. He looked cheerful and eager.

Linda relaxed a bit. 'How much is a ticket to Los Angeles?'

'First class or coach?'

'Coach, I guess. That's the cheapest, right?'

'Right. It's $149.00 one way.' He eyed her overnight bag. 'We have a flight out at 1:15 with a change in Pittsburg. That'll get you into LAX at 3:43 Pacific time.'

'That fast?'

He smiled. 'There's a three hour time difference.'

Linda nodded, feeling like an idiot.

'Round trip?'

'One way.'

'Fine. Name?'

'Thelma Jones.'

He started to punch buttons behind the counter. 'Will you be traveling by yourself, Miss Jones?'

'Just me.'

'Smoking or non-smoking?'

'Non.'

He pressed a few more buttons, then asked, 'Any baggage to check?'

'Is it okay if I just carry this?' Linda asked, lifting her satchel.

'No problem.'

She opened her billfold. 'How much was that?'

'One forty-nine.'

She took out eight twenty-dollar bills.

'Now, you'll have to change planes in Pittsburg. Our flight's on schedule, so you shouldn't have any trouble making the connection.'

With a nod, she handed over the money.

Finally, she had her ticket, her boarding pass, and she could hardly believe it was all so easy. She felt relieved, almost carefree, as she walked in the direction pointed out by the man.

That ended when she saw the people ahead stopping at a gate-like affair and turning over their bags to a uniformed woman. The woman set the bags on a conveyor belt. They vanished inside a metal machine and reappeared on its other side, where the people picked them up after passing through the gate.

'Oh shit,' she muttered.

She turned away. Near the other end of the terminal, she found a restroom. She stood at a sink, washing her hands and brushing the short hair of her wig until she was alone. Then she dumped her pistol into a waste bin.

She passed through security without any trouble.

The taxi crept up the San Diego Freeway in rush-hour traffic. 'Where are they all going?' Linda asked, half to herself.

'Home from work,' the driver said, smiling back at her. 'Home from shopping, home from the airport, Disneyland, the beach. You name it.'

'I've never seen so many cars.'

'Then you've never been to LA. I tell you, one of these days there's gonna be one single car too many coming on, and that'll be it. Nobody'll move. I've got ten days rations in the trunk for the day it happens.'

'Really?'

'Would I kid you?' He swung abruptly into a right-hand lane, slipping into a space barely long enough for the taxi. The car in front slowed down. Linda braced her feet on the floor as the taxi braked. She waited for an impact from the rear. It didn't come. Her left leg ached as she let her muscles loosen. She rubbed it through her dress.

The driver seemed unconcerned about the close call. 'Make sure you take in Grauman's Chinese,' he said. 'They don't call it that anymore, but it's still got the stars' footprints. That's just a few blocks from where I'm dropping you.'

'Okay.'

They moved slowly down a ramp leading onto another freeway. This one looked just as crowded as the other.

Linda glanced at the meter. Seven-fifty. She still had more than two hundred dollars, so . . .

'The Walk of Fame's there, too. You know, the stars in the sidewalk?'

'Yeah, I've heard of it.'

'Some good bookstores along there, too. You into books?'

'A little.'

'Me, I do screenplays. I've picked up some option money, here and there, but I haven't been produced yet.'

'Maybe you should write a book.'

'I've tried. I can't do prose.'

'You write your screenplays in verse?'

He laughed. He didn't explain what was funny, but continued to talk about his writing as he left the freeway and drove up a crowded street named La Brea. Linda felt smothered by the traffic. Often, they had to wait through three cycles of a stop light before getting across an intersection. The amount on the meter continued to rise.

'Hollywood Boulevard,' he finally announced, making a right-hand turn. 'Grauman's, all that, is just up ahead. We'll be turning off, though.'

A few blocks later, he made a left. Then a right onto La Mar Street. He stopped in front of a shabby apartment house, and turned in his seat. Linda gave him thirty dollars. She told him to keep the change.

'Good luck with your poetry,' she said, and left him smiling.

Alone on the sidewalk, she took Tony's letter from her purse. She checked the return address against the numbers beside the building's double glass doors. They matched.

Taking a deep breath, she walked toward the doors. She pulled one open. The lobby seemed dark after the glare outside, and felt slightly cool.

Near the foot of the staircase, she found rows of mail boxes. Each was labeled with two strips of red plastic tape. Her eyes moved swiftly to the strip marked 210, and lowered to the name: A. Johnson.

She'd found him!

She climbed the stairs slowly. At the top, she leaned against the wall. Her breath was coming fast, her heart racing, but not from the exertion.

Shutting her eyes, she saw the naked, cadaverous specter leering down at her through the darkness. The severed head tumbled down the stairs. It bumped her. Its vacant eye peered at her through the gap of her upraised legs. She felt the warm spread of urine. He was coming down, lifting the ax. She felt her terror, her certainty that she would be killed, at last the welcome taste of fresh night air when she made her escape. Then the explosion of pain as the car tore into her.

She gasped and her eyes jerked open as if she'd been startled from sleep.

Her legs were dripping. The insides of her shoes felt slippery. The faded green rug was dark between her feet.

Stunned, she looked down the corridor. At least nobody was around.

She peeled off her sopping panties. With Kleenex from her handbag, she wiped herself dry. She left the panties and tissues in a wet heap, and hurried toward room 210.

All his fucking fault! Everything!

Don't blow it, she warned herself as she raised a fist to strike the door.

She knocked gently.

She waited, hands folded to conceal the blotch on her dress.

The door stayed shut.

She knocked again.

Finally, she gave up. She took the back stairway to the first floor. Stepping out a rear exit, she found herself in an alley. She walked down it, holding the wet part of her dress away from her skin.

In her overnight bag, she carried a change of clothes. She considered ducking between trash bins and ridding herself of the fouled dress.

No. The sun would dry it, soon enough.

She wanted to save the clean clothes for her trip home. Whatever she wore tonight would very likely get messed up with blood.

If she was lucky.

She walked for a long time, sticking mostly to alleys. Finally, she returned to Tony's apartment. She knocked on his door and waited.

Then she went out the front. She crossed the street. Near the end of the block, she sat down on a curb and watched the front of the building and waited.

# TWENTY-FOUR

'OKAY OKAY,' Roger said. 'Ready for the splash shot. It's been a long day. Let's get it right and we'll wrap.'

Jack, crouched on the low roof of the shack facade, gave a nod and pulled the ski mask down over his face. He picked up the ax with both hands.

'Be careful,' Dani called.

'Just get it right,' Roger said, apparently still miffed about last week's foul-up with the shotgun.

Jack's hesitation to blast Ingrid's head. The thought of it made Dani smile. Thank God for such foul-ups. But her good feelings vanished in an instant when she remembered Ingrid's disappearance.

Ingrid, her double.

Tony fondling the dummy, handling its breasts, its buttocks and groin, calling it by her name.

He's just sick enough . . .

'Action.'

Jack leaped from the roof. He landed on his feet in front of the chair where the mannequin of Bill sat with a beer bottle raised to its lips. He swung the ax sideways. It caught Bill across the left eyebrow. The top of the head flew off with a burst of red gore, tumbled and thudded on the porch floor.

'Cut!' Roger called. 'Beautiful. That's a print.'


'Do you want me to go in with you?' Jack asked.

Dani shook her head. 'I'm sure it's all right. He's probably still home licking his wounds.'

'I'd better.'

'If you insist.'

They climbed out of Jack's Mustang and walked toward the front door.

'He didn't pull anything yesterday,' Dani said.

'He didn't dare. I was with you all day.'

She unlocked the door. They stepped inside. The house was silent. They walked through it as quietly as intruders, checking all the windows and doors.

'I guess it's all right,' Jack whispered when they reached the kitchen.

'Then why,' she whispered, 'are we whispering?'

He grinned. 'Beats me,' he said in his normal voice.

Dani glanced at the workroom door. The lock button protruded from its handle. 'Did we leave that unlocked this morning?'

'Might've.'

With a shrug, she stepped around the kitchen table and opened the door. She flicked the light switch. 'Anybody home?' she asked.

'Let's make sure.'

They entered the workroom. It felt hot and stuffy.

'I'll check the back door,' Dani said.

Jack nodded and stepped around the lathe, making his way toward the side window.

As she passed the workbench, Dani picked up the rusted machete. 'Maybe I should keep this with me,' she said. Smiling across at Jack, she waved it overhead.

'Give him forty whacks.'

'Yuck.' She set it down and continued toward the rear door.

'Window's all . . . '

'Jack!' She staggered backwards a step, her gaze fixed on the empty space of wall.

He rushed to her side.

She pointed. 'My life mask. It's gone.'

He was silent for a moment. 'Let's look around. Maybe it's just misplaced.'

She shook her head. She felt weak and dizzy. Jack's hand pressed gently against her back.

'It was here Saturday morning,' he said.

157

'We showed Tony how. He . . . he wants my head on Ingrid.'

Jack mussed her hair. 'As long as he doesn't get the real one.' She tried to smile.

'Honey, it's only a hunk of plaster.'

'It's my *face*. And Ingrid's my *body*. God, I can almost feel him touching it.'

'That's me,' Jack said, pulling her close. He stroked her back. His lips pressed her mouth. She held him tightly. 'We'll get Ingrid,' he finally said.

'How?'

'Tony's bound to show up.'

Jack checked the rear door. Then they left the stifling workroom.

'I'll only be gone an hour,' he said.

'You sure I can't help?'

'You'd be grossed out.'

'Your place can't be *that* messy.'

'If you're afraid to stay here . . . '

'No.'

'I'll just grab enough for one suitcase, and scurry right back.'

When he was gone, Dani chained the front door. She went into the bedroom. Through the glass door, the swimming pool looked shiny and inviting. She could almost feel the cold shock of water. But she was afraid.

Afraid to use her own pool because she was alone and Tony might come through the gate.

'Damn him,' she muttered.

Might as well play it safe, though. Why take chances? Just stay locked up in your cage so the bastard can't get at you . . .

Some cage. A glass house. If Tony wanted, he could get to her in seconds.

With that thought, she convinced herself: she was no safer in the house than outside.

'Clever me,' she muttered.

Laughing softly, she stripped off her sweaty clothes. She went into the bathroom and reached for the bikini hanging over the shower door. It was the skimpy orange one she'd been wearing Saturday. When Tony dropped in.

158

'No way,' she said.

She went to her dresser and took out a green, one-piece suit. Though low cut and backless, it was a vast improvement over the bikini. She stepped into it, pulled it up her legs and lifted the front over her breasts. As she slipped her arms into the straps, she suddenly realised why she was putting it on.

So Tony wouldn't see her in the bikini.

Did she *expect* him to show up?

Yeah. Or why the modest suit?

'Let him,' she said. Picking up a towel, she walked to the door, slid it open and stepped outside. The sun felt warm. A mild breeze blew against her.

'Where'd Jack go?' Tony asked.

Dani's head jerked to the right.

Tony was sitting shirtless on a lounger, hands folded behind his glossy head. The bandages were gone. His face was bruised, blotched and streaked with brown scabs. His left eye was nearly hidden under bulbs of swollen flesh.

Dani stared at him, more confused than alarmed, feeling as if she'd somehow conjured him up. 'How long have you been here?' she asked. The sound of her voice brought back a sense of reality.

'Just a few minutes. I hope you don't mind.'

'You saw Jack leave?'

'No. I just noticed his car wasn't out front.'

'You were coming by anyway?'

He nodded.

'Quite a coincidence.'

'Huh?'

'Jack happens to be gone every time you show up.'

'Yeah. I keep missing him.'

'You're watching the house.' It was not a question.

He looked at Dani as if she were mad.

'And your mother didn't die on Saturday.'

He unlocked his hands from behind his head and leaned forward, frowning. 'She died. Just like I said. Why should I lie?'

'Worked out pretty well, didn't it? I let you stay, I fed you, I took you to the movies. You got your chance to put some moves on me . . .'

'You're crazy!'

'I was crazy to believe you. But, oh, I fell for it, didn't I? You must figure I'm a real push-over. Give me a sob story, I'm putty in your hands. What'll it be today, Tony? Father die? Dog hit by a car? Come on, let's hear it. You wouldn't come without a story for the old softie here.'

He stood up.

Dani backed away as he slowly approached.

'I just can't stay away from you.'

'You do a good job of it when Jack's around.'

'He hates me.'

Reaching behind her, Dani gripped the door handle. 'I want you to leave. Right now.'

He shook his head. 'I can't. I love you. I love you so much.'

'Then do what I want. Go away. Please.'

'I've never loved a woman before. I've never *made* love before.'

'I don't want you, Tony,' she said in a shaky voice.

'Yes you do.'

She suddenly tugged the handle. As the door skidded open, she whirled around and lunged into the bedroom. She tried to jerk the door shut. Tony's body stopped it. He shoved it aside and entered.

Dani staggered backwards. 'Get away,' she gasped.

'I love you. I won't hurt you.'

'Tony!'

'We'll make love. You like that. You do it all the time with Jack.'

'You're not Jack!'

'I'll make you happier than he ever could. You'll see.' He walked toward her.

Dani glanced back. She could try for the bathroom, but its lock wouldn't keep him out for five seconds and she would be trapped. Her only chance was to run for the corridor.

'Don't,' Tony said. 'Don't try to get away. I love you.'

'I hate you!' she shouted, still backing away.

'Oh, don't say that. You know it's not true.'

'Leave me alone!'

'Take off your swimming suit. I want to see you naked. I want to touch you. I want to kiss you all over and . . . ' His body went rigid. He took a quick step back.

Dani spun around and gasped.

In the bedroom doorway stood a big man. He wore jeans, a parka. A blue ski mask covered his head. His gloved hand clutched a machete.

He raised the machete overhead and charged.

Tony darted through the sliding door.

The man rushed past Dani. In silence, he pursued Tony along the side of the pool. Tony reached the redwood fence well ahead of him, leaped, and clambered over the top.

The man came back. He tossed the machete onto one of the lounge chairs, and pulled off his ski mask.

Dani threw herself into his arms.

# TWENTY-FIVE

'ARE YOU all right?' Jack asked.

Dani hugged him tightly. 'He was going to . . .'

'I know.'

'I was so scared. I couldn't have stopped him. Oh God, Jack.'

'It's all right.'

'I couldn't have stopped him,' she sobbed, pressing her face to Jack's shoulder. 'If you hadn't come . . .'

'I was pretty sure he'd take the bait.'

She looked up at Jack. His face was blurry through her tears. 'I don't understand.'

'I expected something like this. I found his hearse on the next street up, so I left my car there and ran back.'

'In costume?' she asked, wiping her eyes.

'I figured I'd give him a dose of his own medicine. When I got here, I saw you outside with him. I went in the workroom for the machete, and by the time I came you were in the bedroom.'

'You mean you never really planned to go to your apartment? You just left me alone to lure him in?'

'That's about it.'

She smiled up at him. 'You're a pretty sneaky fellow, Jack Somers.'

'Takes a sneak to catch a sneak.'

'You could've let me in on your plan, you know.'

'And ruin the surprise?'

'I wouldn't have minded.'

With a smile, he stroked the back of her head. 'Actually, I do have to go to my apartment.'

'What's this, another test to see if Tony shows up?'

162

'I think he's learned his lesson. But just in case I'm wrong, you're coming with me.'

'What about the mess?'

'If you're grossed out, you can shut your eyes.'


He stared at a gray Mercedes parked in front of the apartment building. 'Uh-oh.'

'What?' Dani asked.

'Margot's car.'

'Oh no.'

He swung his Mustang to the curb. 'I guess she didn't take no for an answer.'

'Maybe I'd better wait here.'

Jack grinned at her. 'Scared?'

'I'm not sure I'm up to any more confrontations.'

'Come on.'

'I don't know, Jack.'

'I'm warning you, she might have designs on my body. You'd better come up to protect your interests.'

'Well . . .' Dani shrugged and climbed from the car.

Jack took her hand. 'Don't be nervous.'

'Sure.'

As they climbed the stairs to the second floor, Dani's reluctance grew. Her stomach hurt. Her heart pounded hard. Her hand was sweaty in Jack's grip. 'I don't know about this,' she whispered.

'I haven't seen a good cat fight in ages.'

'Oh wonderful.'

'Don't worry, I won't let her hurt you.'

'You may think this is amusing, but I bet Margot won't.'

'I really should've taken my key away from her. Hope she's not in there wrecking the place.' He slid a key into the lock, turned it, and eased open the door. He leaned into the gap. 'Oh my God,' he muttered. 'Margot!'

Then he shoved the door open wide.

Dani glimpsed a naked woman and quickly turned away. 'I'll meet you in the car,' she said.

Jack grabbed her arm. 'Oh no you don't.'

'You despicable cad.'

'I know,' he said. Grinning, Jack sipped his margarita.

Dani raised herself off the lounge chair and turned it away from the pool's glare. She sat down again, facing Jack.

'Do you still love me?' he asked.

'You're so damned pleased with yourself.'

'I have to admit it, I am.'

She licked the salty rim of her glass, and took a drink. 'You really put me through it.'

'I am rather sorry about that.'

'*Rather* sorry?'

'Will you forgive me?'

'I'll give it some thought.'

Setting his glass aside, he dropped from his chair and knelt in front of Dani. 'Oh please. I humble myself before you.'

'I don't know.'

He pressed his forehead against her knees. His hands moved up her thighs.

'What are you doing?'

'Humbling myself.'

'That's not what it feels like.'

'This is how a cad does it,' he said, and plucked open the bikini strings at her hips.

Dani dumped her margarita on his head. He flinched and cringed, raised his dripping face and grinned. 'Does this mean we're even?'

She smoothed his wet hair. 'Actually, you're a very thoughtful guy in your own perverted way.'

'I know.'

'Have I thanked you?'

'Not yet.'

'Remind me. I'll thank you after dinner.'

They ate pork chops and rice by candle-light in the dining room. When they were done, Jack reminded Dani to thank him.

They each carried a candle down the dark corridor to the bedroom and placed them side by side on the dresser. The mirror

164

caught the flames, made twins of them.

Dani turned to Jack. She caressed his chest, hands roaming over his soft hair, feeling the firm smoothness beneath, thumbs stroking his nipples while he untied the strings behind her neck and back. Her bikini top fell away. She trembled as he touched her breasts, as his fingers slid down her body and plucked the strings at her hips. Then she was naked. A hand was big and warm, moving over her buttocks. Another hand curved over her thigh. Like a breeze, it stirred the hair between her legs. It pressed in. It rubbed. Squirming against it, Dani tugged at Jack's trunks. The hand slid upward, making a wet trail on her belly as she crouched and lowered the trunks to his ankles. She kissed the tip of his rigid penis. Her lips spread over it and she sucked it deep into her mouth.

Then she was on the bed beside Jack, breathless as his tongue thrust into her mouth. He was long and smooth against her. His mouth went away. Kneeling over her, he licked a nipple, squeezed it with his lips, slid a hand down between her legs. A finger dipped into her and stroked.

The doorbell rang.

Jack groaned.

'Wonderful,' Dani muttered.

It rang again.

His mouth lifted off her breast. Dani took hold of his hand to stop it from leaving. 'Never mind the door,' she said.

Neither of them moved as they waited for the doorbell to stop. It kept ringing.

'Persistent bastard,' Dani said.

'I'll see who it is.'

'No, he'll go away.'·

There were moments of silence, but each time that Dani thought the intruder had left, the bell rang again.

'Shit.'

'I wonder if it's our friend,' Jack said.

'He wouldn't show up with you here.'

'I'll be right back. Don't go away.'

Propped up on an elbow, she watched Jack step into his trunks and hurry from the room. When he was gone, she sat up. Sweat

165

trickled down her body. She wiped it off with a sheet.

The doorbell stopped.

She gazed through the fluttering candle light at Jack's gift, and smiled. If not for the interruption, her little 'thank you' might be over by now.

This gave them both a chance to cool off.

When Jack returned, they would start fresh.

She stared at the dark corridor beyond the doorway. She heard no voices, no footsteps.

It shouldn't take him this long.

'Jack?' she called.

No answer came.

Suddenly concerned, she scurried off the bed. She grabbed her robe off a closet hook and rushed to the doorway. Leaning out, she peered down the long corridor. Nothing seemed to move in the darkness.

'Jack?' she asked in a hushed voice.

There was only silence.

She stepped out of the room. Clawing the wall near the door frame, she found the switch panel. Three overhead lamps came on, filling the corridor with light.

No one was there.

She ran to the front door.

Shut.

Racing past it, she scanned the dark living room. The dining room. She rushed around the bar, into the kitchen. Turned on a light. The kitchen was empty. Her bare feet slapped the linoleum floor as she ran to the workroom. It was dark. Reaching in, she flicked a light switch. She stepped through the doorway. Nobody there.

She ran back to the front door and flung it open. She gazed into the darkness.

Nothing moved.

'Jack!' she yelled. 'Jack, where are you?'

When no answer came, she walked over the cool wet grass to the middle of the lawn.

His Mustang was still in the driveway beside her Rabbit. She crossed over to it and peered inside. The car was empty.

She walked down the driveway to the street. Standing by the curb, she looked both ways. There were parked cars, lights shining in the windows of a few houses, but she saw nobody.

Shivering, she drew the robe more tightly around her body and hurried back to the door.

In the kitchen, she took her largest butcher knife from the rack.

*The machete . . .*

But it was out by the pool. She wouldn't go out again.

She turned off the light. Clutching the knife so hard her hand ached, she sat down on the floor. She leaned back against the bar, drew her knees up close, and waited.

# TWENTY-SIX

OPENING HIS eyes, Jack saw blackness. He blinked to be sure they were actually open. A wave of pain crashed inside his head.

He raised a hand to his face, vaguely aware of his elbow sliding on a smooth surface at his side. He thought little of it as he rubbed his temples.

What the hell was wrong with his head?'

He remembered being with Dani. Oh. Right. The doorbell. He'd left her to answer the door. Then he must've gone back.

Christ, his head felt like it might explode.

How the hell many margaritas did he have? Two? And wine with dinner.

Why is Dani's room so dark?

She must have aspirin in the bathroom. He hoped he could get there without tripping over the furniture.

He started to sit up. Something slammed against his forehead. He fell back, dizzy with pain, and grabbed his head with both hands. Cushions of some sort held his elbows in.

As the pain subsided, he poked his right elbow against the obstruction. It sank into padding and struck a hard surface. His left elbow did the same. He raised a fist. Not more than a foot above his face, his knuckles hit wood.

Feeling with both hands, he found that he was boxed in. He braced himself and shoved with all his strength against the lid. The effort sent a tide of pain into his head. He kept on pushing. His muscles quivered with the strain, but the lid didn't give at all. Gasping for breath, he lowered his arms.

This is not good, he thought.

There was a whisper of panic in his mind. He knew he was sealed inside a coffin, the coffin Tony kept in his hearse. When he opened the front door, Tony must have bashed him, knocked him out . . .

*Dani!*

Oh my God, he's going for Dani!

Suddenly, Jack felt motion. Not of the coffin itself, but of the surface on which it rested. Tony, he realised, must be driving him somewhere. Away from Dani's house? So she was safe for now.

Unless Tony had already finished with her.

Christ, why did he have to open the door? Dani had told him not to bother. He should've stayed with her, protected her. Now he was powerless to help. Maybe it was already too late. He saw her sprawled on the floor of her bedroom, naked and bleeding. Dead.

'*No!*' he yelled.

I've got to calm down, he warned himself. There can't be much air in here. Can't waste it. Breathe easily.

The hearse turned, pressing his shoulder to the coffin wall.

You've got to believe he hasn't hurt Dani. He's just taking me out of the picture.

*Just?*

And then he'll go for her, and I won't be around to stop him *unless I get out of this fucking coffin*!

He forced his knees against the lid and shoved it while he pushed with both hands. It didn't yield.

Maybe the side panels aren't so strong. He rolled. There was just enough space for his shoulders. With his back pressed to one padded wall, he thrust against the other side. No good.

As he relaxed his muscles, the coffin jostled him. He pressed himself against the sides again to steady himself.

The car must have gone off the street. From the bouncing, he imagined it traveling over a rutted dirt road or a field.

Where is he taking me?

A cemetery? The thought made a cold, tight place in Jack's stomach.

No. Cemeteries have gates, watchmen. Don't they?

Besides, there isn't one around here. Not that Jack knew of.

Tony wouldn't need a cemetery. Just an isolated spot where

nobody would see him dig a grave.

A grave.

Jesus Christ!

He tried again to force the sides, and then the bouncing stopped. All movements stopped, even the barely perceptible vibration from the car's engine.

For a few moments, nothing happened.

The coffin jerked and rolled with a muffled rumbling sound. The end started down. Jack stretched out his legs to catch himself as he slid on the smooth upholstery. Realising what would happen next, he braced himself up with his elbows. The coffin suddenly dropped out from under him. His head bumped the lid. Then he was slammed down hard. The impact knocked his elbows up, sledged his back, drove his wind out. As he gasped for air, he heard a rapping on the lid.

'Hello in there.'

Tony's voice. It didn't sound distant and muffled. It seemed, somehow, to creep inside the coffin with Jack.

'Cozy?'

Jack lay motionless and said nothing.

'Ever see *Premature Burial*? American International, 1962? One of Corman's best, I think. A real chiller. Me, I can't think of anything much worse than getting buried alive. Drowning, maybe, but that's over a lot quicker. Bury a guy alive and he suffocates real slowly. Has lots of time to think about it. Lots of time. I bet you're already thinking about it. Are you, Jack?'

Jack didn't answer.

'Are you awake in there?' Tony knocked on the lid. 'Hey, are you awake? I don't want you missing this.'

There was a brief silence.

'If you ask me real nice, maybe I'll let you out. Why don't you beg me? Say "Please, oh Chill Master, please let me out. I'm too young to die." No? Well, any last words for Dani? I'll be seeing her later on. I'd be glad to give her a message.'

Jack ached to shout out his rage, to slam his fists through the coffin lid and grab Tony's throat. But he remained silent and didn't move.

Let Tony think he was still unconscious.

170

The bastard thrived on terrifying people. Let him think he failed, at least this once.

The coffin shook, and the foot of it lifted. It was being dragged.

It dropped with a sudden shock.

Something hit the wood above Jack with a soft thud. He felt a trickle on his chest and touched it, rolled it against his skin. Tiny granules. Soil.

More spilled onto him. Jack reached up to the lid. His trembling fingers found a smoothly bored hole.

An air hole.

For a while, he counted the heavy slaps of dirt on the coffin. Even after he lost count, he held his finger to the hole.

Finally there was silence, a heavy, dull silence as black as death.

# TWENTY-SEVEN

THERE WERE no empty spaces in front of Tony's apartment house, so he double-parked. He rushed upstairs.

In his room, he propped the shovel against a wall. He tugged off his shoes and socks, pulled off his soiled pants and climbed into the tub. He turned on the shower. The hot water smacked his skin. Gray streams rolled down his arms, his chest and belly. He let the water hit his face. It felt like fire on his wounds. Quickly, he soaped himself down and rinsed. Then he climbed from the tub.

As he dried himself, he thought about shaving. The two days growth of whiskers made him look grubby. But shaving would be too painful, so he decided against it.

He dumped a pool of cologne into his hand. He splashed it on his cheeks and neck, enjoying the musky fragrance. Then he dabbed some on his penis.

He brushed his teeth.

From his closet, he took a pair of blue slacks and his sport shirt. Not bothering with underwear, he put them on.

He put on clean socks.

He dumped loose soil from his sneakers. Wishing he had a better pair of shoes for the occasion, he slipped them on.

Then he hurried down to his hearse.

Everything was going his way.

Almost everything. Climbing in behind the wheel, he again felt a stir of disappointment about the business with Jack. He must've beaned the jerk too hard. It would've been nice to hear him blubber and beg and scream, but at least he was out of the way. He wouldn't be popping up to ruin the night.

172

**Not this time.**

Tony grinned. It made his lips hurt. He licked them and tasted blood, and laughed.

# TWENTY-EIGHT

THE SUDDEN ring of the doorbell sent a shock through Dani. Her head jerked back, striking a cupboard door. She shoved away from it, and got to her knees.

She was puzzled. She'd expected Tony to break in through the rear of the house, not simply step up to the front door and ring the bell like a casual visitor.

Maybe it's Jack.

But where had he been, all this time?

The bell rang again.

If it were Jack, he would call out.

Tony, all right.

Getting to her feet, she walked around the bar. The knife hilt was slippery. She wiped it with the front of her robe, rubbed her hand dry and gripped it again.

She stopped at the front door. Leaning a shoulder against the frame to steady herself, she took a few deep breaths. They didn't help much; her heart seemed to be knocking the air from her lungs.

'Who is it?' she asked.

'It's just me.'

The strength drained from Dani. She sank to a crouch. 'What do you want?'

'I thought, you know, I'd just drop by and see if you're in.'

'Where's Jack?'

'Oh, isn't he here? His car's outside.'

'Please, what'd you do to him?' Dani didn't like the pleading sound of her voice.

'If he's not here, I don't know where he could be.'

'Tony!'

174

'Maybe he went for a walk. Why don't you let me in, and I'll keep you company till he gets back.'

'Stop *playing* with me!' she shouted. 'I know you've got him!'

There was a long silence.

'Don't be mad, Dani. I didn't hurt him. I just made sure he wouldn't be around. He kept getting in the way, coming between us. I mean, he wouldn't leave us alone. I *had* to get rid of him.'

'What did you do to him?' she whispered.

'Huh?'

'Where is he?' she asked, forcing herself to speak louder.

'He won't bother us. Let me in.'

'No.'

'Don't be this way, Dani. I love you. I won't even try to scare you, I promise. I don't care about that when I'm with you. I just want to hold you in my arms.'

'If I let you in, will you tell me where Jack is?'

'All right.'

Dani straightened up. Holding the knife behind her back, she slipped the guard chain free. She stepped back. She reached out with her left hand, and turned the knob. She swung the door open wide.

Tony, standing on the dark stoop, gazed in at her. He looked strange, almost normal, in slacks and a short sleeved shirt.

All dressed up.

He thinks this is a date.

'Come in,' Dani said.

With a slight nod, he stepped forward. He entered. As he shut the door, Dani's chest constricted. She felt trapped and suffocating. She gasped for air.

'Don't be afraid,' Tony said.

'Where's Jack?'

'We haven't even kissed yet.'

'Tell me.'

Tony shook his head, and took a step toward Dani. She swung the knife from behind her back. She shook its blade at him. 'Tell me where Jack is,' she demanded.

Tony sighed. 'Why don't you forget about him? You have me, now. Forget about Jack. He's nothing.'

She jabbed at his belly. He lurched backwards against the d‹
and flung out his open hands to shield himself. Dani slashed. ‹
blade sliced his left palm.

'*Ow*! Dani! For Godsake, you *cut* me!'

'Tell me where Jack is.'

'All right, all right. God!' He stared at his cupped hand‹
horrified look on his face as blood welled up and spilled over
sides. 'God, you really cut me.'

'I'll do it again. Talk.'

His hand jumped, flinging the pooled blood at Dani's face
flew at her like a tattered red cloth. It splashed her cheeks ‹
eyes. Blinded for a moment, she lashed out wildly with the kn‹
A fist clubbed her left cheek. The impact snapped her h‹
sideways, turned her whole body, and sent her to the floor. ‹
landed on her side. The knife was still in her hand. Hanging o‹
it, she pushed herself to her knees.

Tony kicked her arm out from under her. As she collaps‹
the knife flew from her numb hand.

He grabbed her ankles. He lifted her legs and swung th‹
across each other. Dani tried to clutch the carpet. No use. In
instant, she was forced onto her back. She tried to kick free, ‹
Tony held her feet tightly, bracing each against one hip. ‹
bucked and twisted and squirmed. Her efforts did no go‹
Exhausted, she gave up and tried to catch her breath.

Tony didn't move. He stared down at Dani.

The struggle had loosened her cloth belt. Her robe had fal‹
open. She lifted it from the sides and started to close it over ‹
breasts.

'Don't,' Tony murmured.

She wrapped it tightly across her. Glaring up in defiance, ‹
pressed a hand between her legs.

'You're not being nice.'

'Fuck you,' she gasped.

'This isn't the way it was supposed to be. You were suppos‹
to be sweet and gentle. You weren't supposed to fight me.'

'You wouldn't tell.'

'Huh?' He frowned as if confused.

'I would've been sweet and gentle . . . but you didn't tell.'

'Really?'

'Really. Tell me now. That's all I want. Then I . . . I won't ght you anymore.'

'You'll be nice?'

'I'll be wonderful.' She slid her hand away, uncovering her gina. She spread the robe away from her breasts. 'Tell me.'

'He's in my coffin. Buried someplace.'

'Oh my God,' Dani muttered.

Tony grinned, and blood trickled from his scabbed lips.

'Where?'

He shook his head. 'I'll save that for later.'

'All right.'

'I want you to undress me. Do it the way you undressed Jack the pool Saturday night.'

'You watched?'

'Oh yes. You were so beautiful. You were far away, though. couldn't see as well as I wanted. But the way you slowly dressed him and touched him . . . ' Tony lowered her feet to e floor. 'And then later, when he made love to you in the hirlpool . . . '

'Did it excite you?' Dani asked, standing up.

'Oh yes. But it made me mad. It should've been me.'

'Tonight, it will be you.' Stepping close to him, Dani shrugged e robe from her shoulders. She stood motionless while his eyes andered over her body. He licked a speck of blood from his acked lips. Then he raised his hands. They felt like ice on her oulders. The cut hand was slippery. His fingers trembled as he ressed her. He was breathing hard.

Slowly, Dani unfastened the buttons of his shirt. She untucked and spread it open. His chest was white and hairless, bony as the skin had been stretched taut over a skeleton. Reaching up, e slipped the shirt off his shoulders. He lowered his arms to let fall away.

As she pulled at his belt buckle, his hands slid down to her easts. She went rigid and shut her eyes.

It's all right, she told herself. Don't try to stop him.

The fingers curled around her breasts, squeezing and writhing ke snakes.

She jerked his buckle open. It pulled from her hands as To
crouched. Caressing her buttocks, he kissed her left breast. S
looked down at him. He licked her nipple, sucked it into
mouth, opened wide as if trying to draw in her entire breast. S
felt the painful pulling, the scrape of his teeth, the push of
probing tongue.

'You're hurting me,' she said.

Obediently, he slipped his mouth off the breast. 'I'm sorr
he said. He gave her an apologetic glance, then moved his fa
to the other breast. It was smeared with blood from his har
His tongue circled it, lapping the blood away. Clutching
buttocks, he rubbed it with his face. She felt his whiskers,
stiff touch of his scabs. He pushed an eye against her nipple, a
she felt its quivering lid. His head turned slightly, and he slid t
nipple across his other eye. Then he took it into his mouth.

Dani stroked his head. 'Now,' she whispered. 'I want y
now.'

He stood up. He held her breasts as she unbuttoned his wa
band.

'This is . . . ' He swallowed. 'Better than I ever imagined.'

'Me too.' Dani slid his zipper down. His erection sprang o
Crouching down, Dani lowered his pants. She held them at
knees. Her right hand eased up his thigh.

Tony moaned.

He bellowed when her fist smashed into his scrotum.
staggered backwards. The pants tripped him. He dropped to
rump and fell sideways, curling up and clutching himself.

Dani scrambled for the knife. She spotted it under the cof
table. Dropping to her knees, she reached under and grabbed
Then she hurried back to Tony.

He was still curled up, writhing and groaning.

She knew she could get away while Tony was helpless.
another couple of minutes, though . . .

She raced into the kitchen, threw open the workroom do
and slapped the light switch. On a hook near the window hu
a coil of rope, the remains from what they'd used to tie up
Sandra Blaine mannequin for *Carrion*. She ran for it. The ed
of the workbench gouged her hip. She winced and gritted

teeth against the pain, but didn't stop, Stretching up, she grabbed the rope and yanked it free.

She dashed into the kitchen. Her sweaty feet slipped on the linoleum, but the dining room carpet gave good traction and she sprinted for the living room.

Tony was gone.

# TWENTY-NINE

DANI STOOD on the carpet where, less than a minute ago, the boy had been squirming in agony. Now, only his trousers and a few smears of blood remained to mark the place.

She looped the rope over her head to free her left hand. She scanned the living room, turning slowly. The only light came from the foyer. It reached the area where she stood, casting her shadow over the pale carpet, dimming a short distance beyond and leaving much of the room murky.

Tony would be there. Maybe hiding behind the curtains that stretched across the sliding door and picture windows. Maybe crouched by the sofa or easy chair. Maybe hunched down next to the stereo console. Waiting. Ready to spring at her.

She backed away. Standing under the light, she glanced down the long corridor.

He might even be down there. Waiting inside the guest bathroom or her bedroom.

The knob of the front door pressed cool against her rump. In seconds, she could be outside, racing to a neighbor's house. But that wouldn't help Jack.

Buried alive.

My God, *buried alive!*

How long could he last?

Dani shoved away from the door and walked straight forward. Her shadow moved ahead of her, faded as she left the light behind. She went up the middle of the room, turning, sidestepping, walking backwards, never pausing as she checked the dark places where Tony might be hiding. In the corner, she kicked an armchair against the wall. She ducked to peer under a lamp table. She climbed onto the sofa and walked the length of it, her feet

180

sinking into the soft cushions, her hand trailing through the curtains behind it. At the end, she stepped onto the coffee table. A long stride took her to an overstuffed chair. She leaned over its back. Nobody there. She jumped down. With her back pressed to the wall, she used one hand to pull the draw cord. The curtains slowly skidded open, revealing an expanse of window and the shimmering blue surface of the lighted pool.

Her gaze swept through the room.

'Tony!'

No answer.

She made her way back, pivoting, ducking, peering into shadows behind furniture. In the dining area, she squatted low and scanned the space under the table. There was darkness and a forest of oak legs. She straightened up. She turned around. She stepped to the long side of the bar, planted a knee on a stool cushion and crawled onto the counter top. Inching forward, she looked over the edge and found him.

The coil of rope around her neck stopped swaying.

Tony jerked it hard.

Crying out, Dani braced herself on stiff arms as pain hit the back of her neck like a club. Her head snapped down. The rope scorched her ears, burnt a swath up the back of her head and was gone. Before she could move, Tony whipped it across her face. She threw herself backwards, eyes squeezed shut with pain, and felt another vicious lash. Her right knee left the counter. The oak edge hammered her hip, scraped along her ribs, tore at her breast, caught her under the arm and seemed to shove her away. Her knee knocked a stool over. The side of her ribcage hit another, flipping the stool sideways. She fell on it, her body slamming against the seat edge, the legs and rungs. In a daze, she rolled off it.

She pushed herself to her hands and knees. The knife was gone. She lurched forward, scuttling over the carpet, digging in her toes, shoving away with her fists, trying to stand. With a *whish* and smack, the rope seared her rump. Then she was on her feet. She dodged around the corner of the bar, and ran.

Footfalls and harsh breathing close behind. *Whish!* The rope cut across her back.

She raced past the front door, into the corridor. Then a hand rammed against her back. She flew forward, legs flinging out wildly to stay under her. But it was no use. She hit the carpet chest-first and skidded to a halt.

'You're mine now,' Tony gasped. 'You should've been nice.'

He stepped on her.

He stood on her buttocks with both feet.

'I loved you, Dani.' He bounced, grinding her pelvis against the carpet. 'I never loved anyone else. I think I'll skin you. I'll tie you up and cut your skin off a piece at a time. No. No, I'll use my teeth. Would you like that?' He bounced again.

Dani thrust herself up. The feet shot off her rump. Glancing back as she scurried over the carpet, she saw Tony hit the wall with his shoulder and sprawl backwards, arms flailing.

She dashed down the corridor. Grabbing the door frame, she hurled herself into her bedroom. She slammed the door. Her thumb jabbed the lock button down.


'You can't get away from me!' Tony kicked the door, but it held. 'I'm gonna get you! I'm gonna rip your skin off!'

He stepped back, ran at the door and smashed his shoulder against it. The impact hurled him back.

'I'll *get* you!' he yelled.

Then he raced to the guest bathroom. He flicked on the light, tugged open a drawer under the sink. A fingernail file. It was metal and pointed. He ran to the bedroom door. His hand trembled badly. Then the point scraped into the key hole. He twisted the file and heard a soft, ringing *pop*.

He threw the door open, stepped inside, and shut it.

Except for the flames of two candle stubs on the dresser, the room was dark.

'Where *are* you?' he sang. 'I'm gonna *get* you.'

He stared at the bed: the coverlet heaped at its foot, the top sheet thrown back, the pillows crooked. She must've been on it earlier with Jack. Making love. By candle light.

Rushing forward, he dropped to his knees and peered into the darkness under the bed.

Not there.

He stood up, turned around. The door to the master bathroom was shut.

'Well well, Dani.' As he took a step toward it, he heard the sound of a heavy splash.

He whirled. He charged past the end of the bed and batted the curtains aside. The glass door was open. The water in the lighted pool still trembled from the impact.

He ran to the pool's edge.

He stared.

The body was face-up in the deep water near the diving board, rigid as a corpse, sinking slowly toward the bottom.

'Dani!'

Her eyes gazed up at the surface as if entranced by the view. Her mouth was wide open.

Tony sidestepped along the rim of the pool.

God, she looked beautiful, the lights shimmering on her naked body, her hair drifting as if stirred by a strange wind.

Tony wanted her so badly.

But he couldn't go into the water, not even for Dani. Suppose it was a trick, and she grabbed him and held him under . . .

If it's a trick, she'll come up for air.

But she didn't.

She sank to the bottom.

She blurred and streaked as tears filled Tony's eyes. 'Oh Dani,' he whispered.

Then pain split his head.


Tony winced. His head throbbed. He wanted to hold it, but when he tried to raise his hands, they wouldn't move. He opened his eyes.

He was outside, facing Dani's house, lashed to the aluminum frame of a patio chair.

His head pulsed as he looked from side to side. At first, he saw no one in the darkness. Then a pale figure stepped out from behind the distant barbeque.

It walked slowly toward him.

It was a naked woman, her skin pale in the moonlight.

She held a machete in one hand, a cannister in the other.

'Who are you?' Tony gasped.

'You know me.'

She was near enough for the pool lights to flutter dimly on her face.

'Get away!'

She shook her head. She tossed the machete aside, its blade clattering on the concrete. 'I almost used the blade,' she said. 'I would've, but I need some information.'

She shook the cannister in her left hand. Tony heard sloshing liquid.

Charcoal lighter!

She flicked up the plastic cap. Without another word, she squirted the fluid onto him. It came out in a thin stream, splashing over his shaven head, running down his face. It felt cold except when it touched his wounds, and then it burned.

'You can't do this!'

She said nothing. The stream stopped for a moment. The can made a hollow, buckling sound, and squirted again. She moved it back and forth, criss-crossing his chest, his belly.

'What do you want?'

The can made another popping sound. She aimed the fluid between his legs. It matted his pubic hair, splattered his limp penis, trickled down his scrotum.

She walked away.

'Where're you going!'

'To get the matches.'

'No! Please! Oh my God, don't! I'm sorry! I was just kidding about skinning you! Honest! I'm sorry! I'll leave you alone, I promise! I'll do anything! PLEASE!'

She stopped and turned.

'Tell me where to find Jack.'

# THIRTY

SHE LEFT Tony tied to the chair. Rushing across her bedroom, she tossed the machete to the floor. She grabbed her handbag from the dresser and blew out the candle flames.

In the living room, she scooped her robe off the floor. She shoved her arms into it as she raced for the workroom. Propped against the side wall beside the rake was a spade. She grabbed it.

Then she was outside, sprinting across the cool wet grass, the robe fluttering behind her like a cape. At her car, she jerked open the handbag. She felt inside for the key case, couldn't find it, crouched and dumped the contents on the driveway. She snatched her keys and billfold from the heap. Clamping the billfold under her arm, she snapped open the key case. She found the car key. It kept missing the lock hole. She held her hand steady with her other hand, and the key slipped in.

She twisted it, tugged open the door and threw the shovel across the back seat. She flung herself behind the wheel and managed to fit the key into the ignition. The engine sputtered to life. She rammed the shift into reverse, remembered to shut the door but forgot to release the emergency brake. When she popped the clutch, the car lurched and died.

Dani whimpered.

She took the brake off. The car started rolling backwards. She turned the key and gunned the engine and sped down the driveway.


Tony, still sobbing from the ordeal, squirmed on the chair. The ropes burnt into his arms and feet as he struggled. Though his arms seemed bound securely, he felt some give around his feet. He strained against the ropes. He kicked. The bindings seemed

185

to loosen. Pressing his right ankle against the aluminum tubing of the chair leg, he drew his foot up. His heel squeezed out! He drew his knee up, and his foot slipped free.

Using it to shove at the rope wrapped around his left foot, he had little trouble pulling loose.

He thrust himself forward. The chair tipped onto its front legs. He stood, hunched over the chair pressed to his back and rump, and took a waddling step.

If he could just get inside, get to the knife or machete . . . If he just had enough time, he knew he could cut himself free.

Sweat and charcoal lighter streamed down his body as he took another step toward the house.


Dani waited at the intersection with Laurel Canyon Boulevard. She moaned in frustration as the cars sped by. 'Come *on*,' she muttered, pounding the steering wheel with her palm.

Finally, there was a break in the traffic. She shot out, tires whining as she swung to the left. Her foot shoved the accelerator to the floor.

Thank God, the field where Tony left Jack wasn't far away. Maybe a five minute drive.

Five minutes.

Each second must seem like forever, trapped in a coffin.

How long could the air last? Not very long. Jack might already be . . .

'Hang on,' she said. 'Please.'

The traffic light on Mulholland turned red. The cars in front of Dani slowed down, stopped. She crept up close to the tail of the Rolls in front of her, pushed the brake pedal down, pressed her forehead to the steering wheel and wept.


Tony had only taken a few short steps toward the sliding door of Dani's bedroom when a voice said, 'Hello.' His head jerked sideways.

A girl stepped away from the gate at the far side of the house. She wore a pale dress.

'Help me,' Tony called.

'Sure,' she said. 'I'll help you.'

Something about the voice sent a chill through Tony. He tried to straighten up. The chair hit the backs of his knees. They buckled and he fell. The chair caught him, scooted back, tipped, but not enough to throw him over.

Just this side of the barbeque, the girl paused. She squatted and stood up again. 'I've been watching you,' she said, slowly walking closer. 'You had a very close call.'

'The woman's nuts. She was gonna kill me.'

'I'm glad she didn't.'

'Untie me?

'I don't think so.'

'Please?'

She shook her head. In the wavering light from the pool, her face looked familiar. 'Who are you?'

'Don't you remember? The old Freeman house?'

His heart thundered. He could barely breathe, but managed to gasp out, 'Linda?'

'You *do* remember.'

'Wha . . . what are you doing here?'

She didn't answer.

'Where'd you come from?'

'Your hearse.'

Twisting his head as far as he could, he saw her stoop down and pick up the tin of charcoal lighter.

'Linda!'

She stepped in front of him. She shook the container. In her left hand was a box of matches.

'Oh Jesus, don't.'

He kicked at her, but she simply stepped to the side of the chair, out of reach.

Fuel squirted onto his head.

'No! I never hurt you! Please! God, Linda, don't! I never hurt you! I never hurt *anyone*!'

187

The car bounced under Dani as she sped over the grassy field. She steered between two trees, turned sharply right to avoid another, and her headlights swept across the coffin.

It was resting on the ground, no more than twenty feet ahead. Not buried at all!

She leapt from the car and ran. Undergrowth stabbed her bare feet, bushes lashed her legs. A root tripped her. She fell sprawling and scurried up and ran and dropped to her knees beside the coffin. Her hands thrust into the piles of dirt on top. She flung her arms back and forth, smashing through the loose soil. It rained against her. She spit to clear her mouth. Then the lid was clear.

She pounded on it. 'Jack! Jack!'

No answer.

Along the rim of the lid were half a dozen metal wing-bolts. She grabbed one and began to unscrew it.


A match flared, casting grotesque shadows over Linda's face.

'No! Come *on*!' Tony rammed his feet against the concrete, shoving his chair backwards a few inches.

Linda puffed out the match.

'Please! I never meant any harm!'

She struck another match. She took a step toward him. Whimpering, Tony thrust his chair further back. Linda flicked the match. Its flame drew a bright, curving mark through the air, went dark, and landed near his feet.

He scooted back.

Another match burst to life.

'*Please!*'

'Scared?' Linda asked, holding out the match.

'I'll do anything!'

'You've already done too much.' The flame burned close to her fingers. 'Tell me you're scared.'

'I'm *scared*!'

She shook the match out, and lit another. 'I was so scared I pissed myself.'

'Okay!' His muscles seemed too tight.

Linda struck another match.

'I'm trying!' Then a hot stream was shooting out, splashing his legs. 'There! See?'

'Isn't it fun?' Linda asked, and tossed the match. The brilliant tear of flame arced toward him.

Tony rammed his heels into the concrete. The chair jumped backwards. The match fell on his lap and he almost laughed in spite of the searing sting because it had gone out an instant before it touched him.

But he didn't laugh.

He shrieked.

He seemed to fall forever, screaming and kicking at the sky. Then the water silenced him.


Dani tossed aside the final bolt and tugged at the coffin lid. She raised it a bit. Her fingers slipped and it thudded down. She grabbed it again and lifted. This time, it felt strangely light. It slid off, and she saw why it had moved so easily.

Jack had helped.

He sat up.

Dani threw her arms around his head, hugging it to her breasts and sobbing.

'I can't breathe,' said his muffled voice.

Dani released him. Taking his arm, she helped him climb from the coffin. 'Why didn't you answer me?' she asked.

He shrugged. 'Thought I was dreaming. I was having a fine dream till you dropped the lid.'

'Sorry.'

'I'll forgive you.' Jack pulled her against him. His powerful body began to shake, and she heard him sobbing, too.

For a long time, they held each other.

# THIRTY-ONE

'I GUESS he never really intended to kill me,' Jack said. 'Other
wise, he wouldn't have drilled the air hole in the top. He must've
cleaned it off after he piled the dirt on.'

'Thoughtful of him,' Dani muttered. She slowed down, and
turned onto Asher Lane. 'What'll we do with him?'

'Let the cops take care of it. Assault and battery, attempted
rape, that oughta be enough to put him away for . . .'

'Oh my God!'

She stared ahead at the empty length of curb in front of her
house.

The hearse was gone.

Jack squeezed her thigh. 'Don't worry. They'll get him.'

'I . . . it's just that . . . I hoped it was over.'

'It's all right.'

She pulled onto the driveway beside Jack's Mustang. Climbing
out, her foot came down on lipstick and a compact. She squatted
down and started to load her handbag. Jack knelt beside her and
helped. Then he put an arm around her. They walked to the
front door.

The house was silent, and dark except for the corridor lights.

Dani frowned. She pointed.

Tony's blue slacks were draped over the back of a nearby
chair, the pocket linings hanging out like pale tongues.

'He must've been in quite a hurry,' Jack said.

They stepped over to the bar. As Jack phoned the police, Dani
picked up the two bar stools she'd knocked over. She started to
make drinks.

Jack finished.

Dani placed a vodka and tonic in his hand.

'I want to propose a toast,' he said, staring at her with solemn eyes. 'To Ingrid.'

'To Ingrid. The nicest gift anyone ever gave me. And certainly the most useful.'

They clinked their glasses and sipped.

'You never finished thanking me,' Jack said.

'I'll have to thank Bruce, too. I feel so awful, giving him a hard time like that. I as much as called him incompetent for misplacing her that way.'

'He was a good sport. Kept his cool. Didn't give me away.'

Dani nodded. 'Well, why don't we go ahead and fish her out?'

They went outside. They walked to the edge of the pool, and Dani clutched Jack's arm.

Neither spoke.

They stared down into the water.

Tony was there, hands still lashed to the patio chair, staring up at them from the bottom of the pool. Ingrid was there beside him, face down. One of her arms was stretched out, though Dani was sure they'd been at her sides when she threw the mannequin into the pool.

The hand of the reaching arm, probably urged by the currents of the filtering system, had found its way to Tony's throat.

'Let's go back inside,' Jack whispered.

They turned away, holding hands tightly, and walked toward the house.

# THIRTY-TWO

'HI MOM? . . . Yes, it's me . . . Sure, I'm fine . . . I flew to Chicago . . . Yes, I'm coming home. I realised I was just being silly, running off like that. I mean, what are the chances the killer'd come after me? Yes, I love you, too. Give my love to Dad and Bob . . . I'll see you tomorrow.'